Linda & Ted –
Thank you
your wisdom and
knowledge –

Please enjoy
The "Drummer"

Burr A
9/9/13

THE DRUMMER

by Burr B. Anderson

authorHOUSE®

AuthorHouse™
1663 Liberty Drive
Bloomington, IN 47403
www.authorhouse.com
Phone: 1-800-839-8640

© 2013 Burr B. Anderson. All rights reserved.

No part of this book may be reproduced, stored in a retrieval system, or transmitted by any means without the written permission of the author.

Published by AuthorHouse 1/2/2013

ISBN: 978-1-4772-9683-7 (sc)
ISBN: 978-1-4772-9682-0 (hc)
ISBN: 978-1-4772-9753-7 (e)

Library of Congress Control Number: 2012923115

Any people depicted in stock imagery provided by Thinkstock are models, and such images are being used for illustrative purposes only.
Certain stock imagery © Thinkstock.

This book is printed on acid-free paper.

Because of the dynamic nature of the Internet, any web addresses or links contained in this book may have changed since publication and may no longer be valid. The views expressed in this work are solely those of the author and do not necessarily reflect the views of the publisher, and the publisher hereby disclaims any responsibility for them.

For Kyle, Kristopher and Zachary Anderson, three wonderful children.

Acknowledgements

To Nancy, who has stood at my side for a wonderful thirty-eight years, while I focused on business, art and writing.

To Mike Anderson, a superb trumpet player and Tom Jacobson, a Pacific Northwest guitar legend, for their professional insight into the world of rock n' roll.

To Deputy Chief Ward Smith of the Placentia Police Department and Sergeant Stewart McCarroll of the Brea Police Department for their superb knowledge of police procedures.

To the members of the Anderson Literary Solutions LLC editorial board; Jim Clary, Larry King, Dan Martin, Craig Mendenhall, Jerry Reilly, Jack Taylor, Craig Voegele and Connie Zittel.

To the professional staff at Authorhouse, whose expert follow-up turned the manuscript into a final product.

To Robert Quill Camp who served as copy editor and did a fantastic job of cleaning up the manuscript.

Chapter 1
Villa Park, CA

HE TURNED THE CORNER at Mesa Drive and walked in the direction of Canyon Circle. This was the third time that he had been on Canyon Circle and after a hundred visits to this street on Google Satellite Maps—he felt like he was in his own neighborhood. The target house was just a few homes ahead and was on the right side of the quiet street. It was a typical Villa Park home, ranch style, on a winding street with no sidewalks. Sunset had been several hours earlier, and the sky was partially cloudy. His right hand went deep into his jacket's pocket as he fingered the plastic bag.

Villa Park is the smallest incorporated city in Orange County, California. Completely surrounded by the City of Orange, Villa Park is only a little more then two square miles in size. The city does not have its own police department, but has its public safety needs served by the Orange County Sheriff Department.

A final glance around the neighborhood indicated that he was alone on Canyon Circle. After taking a few more steps he spotted the boxwood hedge and large trunk of a palm tree that he had already selected as a staging area. Trying to be as casual as possible, he stepped behind the hedge and found himself positioned behind the palm and finally out of sight.

He pulled the plastic bag from his jacket and spread its contents on the dirt between the five-foot hedge and palm tree. As he knelt down on the piece of plastic that had been in the bag, he felt the pressure from the silencer taped to his thigh under his faded wrangler jeans. Almost 8 inches long, the AAC Evolution suppressor would lower the sound of a gunshot by about 40 decibels. He mentally reviewed his checklist - preparation, staging, the hit, escape, and evidence destruction.

From his hiding spot he had a clear view of the front door and at the same time he could see down Canyon Circle. All was clear. Dogs were not going to be an issue.

Using a prepaid cell phone he had phoned the Dupree home last week and identified himself as an officer with Orange County Animal Care. He had questioned the homeowner about dogs in the home that needed a current license. Satisfied that dogs were a non-issue, he had pulled the sim card and burned the phone and card in his barbecue.

Working in the shadows of the large palm tree, he pulled the silencer from his left pant leg and in a calm and deliberate manner he organized surgical gloves, three envelopes and a cell phone. After giving the street another glance, he pulled a Glock 37 from his Galco shoulder holster.

He liked the Glock 37 because it gave him the punch of a .45 caliber but had a grip that was smaller than most .45 cal. handguns. When he put on the gloves he was careful to pull them up and over his right coat sleeve. There probably is not a person left on earth who does not understand gunshot residue. He screwed the Evolution suppressor to the barrel of the Glock without any problems. He gathered up the tape and plastic bag and gave the area a final clean up.

Now, standing behind the palm, he tucked the three envelopes under his arm while he opened the prepaid cell. His right hand carefully held the pistol and its ten rounds of 200 grain Speer Gold Dot 45GAP ammo.

Anticipating that it would be difficult to use the small prepaid with gloves, he had earlier entered the Dupree home number into the speed dial. After pushing the 2 key and the Send button, he took a deep breath and slowly exhaled to bring his heart rate back down. In just a few seconds old man Dupree would answer his phone. Other then an involuntary tick, which caused his head to jerk to the right, he was ready.

Chapter 2
Fred Dupree Home

HIS DEN WAS DECORATED more as a shrine to the past, than as a room used for entertainment. Ever since his wife died, Fred had not been into entertaining. Truth be told, he had not been into anything. His son would stop by every couple of weeks to help his father with minor home maintenance and to make sure that he was taking his hydrochlorothiazide for his high blood pressure. His home, located in Villa Park California, was now a little large for a widower. The kitchen, bedroom and den were the only rooms that Fred used. Fred reached over with his right hand and grasped the Waterford glass that contained a Cadillac Margarita. Even at seventy-two, he could still build a world-class drink. Two ounces of middle grade tequila, six ounces of Baja Bob mix, and three quarters of an ounce of Grand Marnier - shake with ice, pour over ice and then top with Patron Silver. Even in retirement, Fred always said, "It only takes ten percent more to go first class."

Bonney's cancer had ended a fairy tale life. His left hand scrolled through the cable news channels while his eyes drifted to a bookshelf of old mementos and memories.

He and Bonney had gotten married while he was working in Tacoma, Washington with Asarco. For most of the eight years at Asarco he had used his University of Washington Engineering degree to test and recommend procedures to reduce the arsenic in the neighboring city of Ruston. Arsenic was a byproduct of Asarco's smelting business.

Bonney and Fred had dated for a year before getting married. Their time in Tacoma was filled with wonderful memories. It was almost a ritual that every Friday night they would drive down 6th Avenue and pull into the Frisko Freeze Burger joint.

Fred's experience in Tacoma with environmental issues opened the door to an opportunity with the EPA. The era of Superfunds and the government's commitment to clean up toxic sites gave Fred and Bonney a new career in Portland, Oregon. As the 90's approached, Fred saw a shift in environmental focus from water issues to air quality. He and his wife pulled up stakes and relocated to Southern California. Fred formed Dupree Environmental Solutions, a company specializing in air testing and pollutant mitigation. Fred sold the firm only one year prior to Bonney's cancer diagnosis. His wife's battle with cancer was courageous and lasted fourteen months.

It had now been three years and he had not yet found substantial activities to occupy his time. His son had recently suggested that he buy a dog. The house was certainly large enough and like most Villa Park homes he was situated on a half-acre fenced-in lot. Home security was another reason to give the idea serious consideration. Villa Park was a very safe city, but Fred knew that you can never be too security conscious.

The ringing of his phone jarred him away from his rambling thoughts. As Fred picked up his portable phone, he also clicked his TV to mute.

"Fred, this is Robert Bishop down the street. The post office messed up and gave me some of your mail, three letters actually. My son is coming over to drop off your mail…. Sorry Fred, got to go—have another call ringing in."

Fred Dupree took one more sip of his drink and returned it to the drink holder in his Lazy Boy chair. The little lever by his right hip electronically lowered the chair's leg rest. Fred stood up and started walking down the hallway that connected to the front door entryway.

The electronic doorbell started playing *Ave Maria*. The name Robert Bishop did not remind him of a neighbor he knew, but that was not a surprise to him, as there had been several homes on the street that had recently sold.

In the old days, he thought, the postman knew all the homeowners and it was very rare to get the mail mixed up. He saw the outline of his neighbor's son through the doors beveled glass. He pushed in the alarm code to disarm the system and opened the door.

Fred heard the visitor say, "Hi," and then he saw the man's left hand reach out and hand him three envelopes. A second later he saw the man's right hand come from his back holding a large hand gun—at the same time as he felt himself being pushed backwards into the house. The push was so hard that he lost his balance and crashed against an antique chair and landed on his back on the hard travertine floor.

The man said something about just wanting a TV. Looking up, he saw the man close the front door, step over him and aim the gun at his head. Within a fraction of a second, a bullet blasted into the front of Fred Dupree's head, creating a tunnel of pulverized brain tissue and leaving a three-inch hole in the back of his head.

Mr. Dupree felt no discomfort because within a second the .45 caliber bullet had transferred its kinetic energy into his skull and exited along with a fair share of bone and brain particulate.

Chapter 3
Villa Park Dupree Home

THE KILLER STEPPED AWAY from the body and spotted the shell casing still spinning in a little circle on the travertine tile floor. Even though he knew the gun was clean and not traceable to him, his system was to try and recover as much potential evidence as possible. After placing the brass in his pocket he turned his attention to the inside of Dupree's house and listened carefully for any sound that would alert him that the shot had been heard. He heard nothing, and he then watched the pool of blood grow in size and start to run down the grout lines that formed nice diamond shaped patterns between each floor tile.

Prior to the head-shot he had said to Fred, "Don't worry I won't hurt you, I just want your TV." He thought it was important to always give the victim hope—it keeps them from getting aggressive and trying to be a hero. Stepping back a few feet, he raised the gun until it was once more pointed at Fred's head. He remembered that this gun had the NY2 trigger spring. Instead of the standard 5.5-pound pull, this gun had a pull more like that of a revolver: 7 pounds at the start that gradually increased to 11 pounds. When the trigger traveled a half-inch the trigger pull was at 11 pounds. After the gun discharged, it became clear that a third shot was not going to be needed.

He felt no emotion as he looked down at the body and took in the damage that the two bullets had done to the head. Even though he was amped up from the surge of adrenaline, he knew that he must control the dozens of random thoughts that were now jumping around in his mind. "Dust" is what he called any distraction to his clear analytical thinking. Another twitch or tick caused his chin to jerk toward his right shoulder.

He knew he was not normal, and it had been his ability to minimize the dust that had kept him free from the fucking cops for the last five years. Mental discipline would keep the dust from distracting him from his system of lists. He reviewed his checklist: preparation, staging, approach, the job, cleanup, escape, and evidence destruction.

Unscrewing the silencer from the Glock allowed more dust to enter his head. What is the difference, he thought, between a myth and an urban legend? There is never the pink mist from a head-shot. The legend is that when the bullet tunnels through the brain and blasts out the back of the skull it creates this big cloud of pink mist. His recollections of his last three kills were that he didn't remember any pink cloud. Just like the green flash that is supposed to happen when the sun finally sets out in the ocean - or the myth that... "Stop!" he said out loud to himself. He needed clear thinking for the cleanup.

He retrieved the envelopes that had fallen and the last shell casing with the utmost care. Yes, he said to himself, I am back on my game. Dust is not going to interfere with my system. He then said in a low whisper, "It is time to fuck with the brains of the dickheads from the crime scene department." He pulled a little plastic bag from his back pocket and carefully removed three items. He started to chuckle to himself as his gloved fingers selected a suit coat button he had stolen from a Goodwill store. Still laughing, he flipped it near the hand of dead Fred.

He then selected some toilet paper he had grabbed from a Northern California rest stop. Of course he had wiped the paper around the back of a toilet to pick up a bunch of random DNA. The paper he tossed out of sight near the front door frame. Lastly he took three decoy shell casings he had brought and dropped them near the spots where he had picked up his own spent casings. No dust in his head now, he was on top of his game.

Checklist; think clear. The gun was back in the holster and the silencer was taped to his thigh. Looking carefully at the floor he saw no footprints, just the ever-widening pool of blood and pieces of brainshit.

With a gloved hand he made a small opening in the curtain next to the door and carefully studied the front yard. It was clear. He was able to open the door far enough without having to move Fred's feet. He then stepped out quietly into the beautiful California night.

Chapter 4
Orange County Boy's & Girl's Club Gig

"WE ARE NEAR THE end of this gig, Forrest."

Forrest Dupree stole a quick look at the small clock that was attached to his floor tom, and gave Leon a nod of okay. It was 11:25 PM and it was time for the Purple Cinnamon to finish the evening with the final three. Leon Coyne was the band's bass player and had been with Purple Cinnamon for six years. A simple newspaper advertisement was how Forrest had found Leon. When Coyne lit up his bass, Forrest had thought that he was listening to The Who and bassist John Entwistle. Six years later, Coyne still played with the same intensity that he did when he first auditioned for Forrest.

"Final three," Forrest announced as he reached down and grabbed the charts for Purple Cinnamon's last three songs of the evening. This was the third year that they had played for the Boys and Girls Club fundraiser. He liked the gig because the band got a big break when the event organizers brought up the auctioneer to run their live auction. They should be happy this year, he thought, they had one guy bid $3,700 for a suite at Angels Stadium for a Yankees and Angels ballgame.

One, two and three taps of his stick on the edge of the snare was the start of "Every Breath You Take."

Every breath you take

Every move you make

Every bond you break

Every step you take

I'll be watching you...

Leatha was on her game tonight and her light rasp gave Sting's music just the right touch. Leon had used to vocal this piece, but every once in a while, Forrest would get ground on by a jerk who said they should not play a stalking song. After he gave the vocals to Leatha the complaints stopped.

Forrest formed Purple Cinnamon eight years earlier, and the band had had their present members for the last two years. As Leatha pounded the keys and sang away, Forrest stole a glance at the lead guitarist. Shaun Watanabe and Forrest had started the band, and Shaun split his life between coaching baseball and being P.C.'s lead guitar.

They referred to the band as either P.C. or The Cinnamon. Originally Forrest and Shaun wanted to call the band The Dog's Breakfast, because he and Shaun had heard of the expression and thought it would be a cool name. After a couple of months they found out that another group was called The Dog's Breakfast, so they changed the name to Dog's Dinner. The group then did a Google search and discovered that Dog's Dinner was also being used.

The chart for the next to the last song was ready to go as Leatha brought home "Every Breath You Take."

I'll be watching you...

I'll be watching you...

That night Purple Cinnamon did not get through their third set of twelve songs. Forrest wanted the band to stay on top of about fifty songs and usually do three sets with twelve songs per set. The Cinnamon would add one, maybe two songs each month and drop the ones they were sick of. It looked like about half of the crowd had left and the East Room of the Richard Nixon Library was feeling empty. The room was a replica of the East Room in the White House. With about eight couples on the dance floor for Every Breath, he wondered how many would hang in there when they kicked it up a notch.

Shaun took the lead as they jumped into *Love Shack*. The goal of the members of Purple Cinnamon were to finish a gig on a high note. The final three was designed to bring the evening to a strong close, one that assured a re-booking. *Love Shack* was originally performed in 1989 by the alternative rock band The B-52's.

That night, Shaun on guitar and Leatha on keyboard were working very well together. Forrest liked to see how well he could get his bass drum to be hitting with Leon's bass guitar. It appeared to Forrest that several more couples were coming alive and moving to the dance floor.

"Let's bring it home Purple Cinnamon!" Leon shouted while Leatha flipped a bunch of buttons on the Roland keyboard, so it would have the synthesizer sound of Van Halen. Shaun was ready to give his axe a big workout. Many rock n' roll historians have said that Eddie Van Halen's long guitar solo in their band's song "Jump" was the best guitar solo he ever wrote. Forrest saw that Leatha was ready, so he gave P.C. a start for the night's final song.

…Ah, I might as well, jump. Jump!

Might as well jump

Go ahead, jump. Jump!…

When the song reached a little over two minutes, Shaun sprang into action with the song's signature guitar solo and rocked for almost a full minute. Forrest never let up and hammered the toms and cymbals right up to the final beat.

"Before I break down my kit, I want to locate the guy who should have our check." explained Forrest. Forrest Dupree was not only Purple Cinnamon's drummer, but he was considered the band's business manager. Dupree was without a doubt, the most striking member of P.C. First of all, he was very good looking. What made him stand out was his bleached blond hair that he wore short and spiked up with a little gel. Add his dark brown circle beard and nearly everyone did a double take. Many of the band's followers said that Drummer Dupree reminded them of a famous T.V. chef

He was able to locate the Club's Executive Director and picked up the band's check. Reggie Wilhite was well known in North Orange County and it seemed that he ran a good operation at the Boys & Girls Club. "How did you do at the live auction?" asked Forrest.

"Thanks for asking. As you saw, we went with a professional auctioneer this year, and I think it was a good move. One of the board members thought we brought in thirty two thousand, just from the live auction. By the way, thanks for letting our people use all your microphones and amps for the auction and announcements."

"That is why you pay us the big bucks my friend." replied Forrest. "Reggie, I need to get back and pack away all our equipment before President Nixon personally kicks us out of his library.

The Richard M. Nixon Presidential Library was a key attraction for the City of Yorba Linda. The actual house that he was born in was located on the site along with the famous Sikorsky Sea King helicopter that was used by Kennedy, Johnson, Nixon and Ford.

"Hey Forrest, when we get all packed up, do you think security will let us have a couple of drinks inside Marine One?" asked Leon.

"I will tell the security guard that we won the helicopter at the silent auction.," replied Forrest.

Chapter 5
Villa Park Police Station

CHIEF GENITO DROVE HIS unmarked SUV West on Santiago Blvd., and then turned right into the Villa Park Ralph's shopping center. As the Chief passed Rockwell's Cafe and Bakery he thought about the black and bitter fresh coffee he was about to enjoy. At six in the morning he had his choice of parking spots at the Villa Park City Hall. Thank god, he thought as he poured his six foot five inch frame out of the Chevy Tahoe, that the department had issued him an SUV instead of a standard deputy sedan. Vince Genito did a quick look in the rear view mirror to make sure his silver gray hair was all in place—he had always been a big believer that you lead by example, and personal grooming was high on the list. His signature in the department was the sharp crease he always had on his slacks.

"Hi Carol, what is the special of the day?"

"Good morning, Chief. Big cup or medium?"

"Large this morning, and I may be back for more. Today looks like paperwork—it's budget time," replied Chief Genito.

Twenty-year sheriff veteran Vince Genito was a lieutenant with the Orange County Sheriff Department. Twelve cities in Orange County California contracted with the sheriff department to be their police department. Because Villa Park is one of the twelve cities, and because of its size, a sheriff lieutenant is put in charge. Lt. Genito had been the Villa Park Police Chief for three years.

"Chief, it's Tuesday, and that means our usual Italian entrees," said Carol. Carol opened Rockwell's at six each morning then moved to the baking kitchen to oversee the preparation of some of the best cakes and desserts in Southern California.

As Genito headed out the door he said to Carol, "I may surprise my wife and pick up one of those tiramisu cakes on my way home."

Carol replied, "I will keep one in the back for you just in case."

The Chief passed by his SUV and hit his key lock one more time. Lt. Genito not only had the responsibility of public safety in Villa Park, but he was also in charge of the seventy-one little unincorporated areas in North Orange County. His official job description was Chief of Public Services, Villa Park and North Patrol Commander.

Villa Park's contract with the OCSD called for one patrol car to be on patrol at all times, so the Chief did not expect to see that day's deputy parked at the V.P. substation that morning. As the Chief settled into his desk he reflected on how good this current duty assignment was. He had done very well on his last evaluation and knew that a promotion to Captain might be in the near future. If he were to be promoted to Captain he would have to give up his current position as Villa Park Chief of Public Safety. The Orange County Sheriff Department contracted with twelve cities and Villa Park had the lowest crime statistics of all twelve. With a total population of about 6,000 the city had a burglary, larceny or theft about every three days.

"Good morning, Vince. Do you want to catch a cup of coffee later this morning and look over my numbers for our C.E.R.T. equipment request to the council?" asked City Manager Herb Blansett.

"Herb, I will be good in about one hour, how about Rockwell's?" answered Chief Genito. C.E.R.T. stood for Community Emergency Response Team and Genito knew that the city would have to buy a bunch of two way radios for all of the volunteers who went through the approximately twenty hours of training.

After meeting with the City Manager, Chief Vince Genito placed a call to a fellow Rotarian about a forthcoming past presidents luncheon at Rockwell's. It was going to be a busy week; the day after the Rockwell's luncheon was the annual singing competition that was to take place between students of Villa Park High and Lutheran High. Thank god crime was very low in Villa Park, thought the Chief.

Chapter 6
Villa Park Dupree Home

PHILLIS PETRILLO HAD NEVER been a morning person. Her favorite saying was, "Is it light outside at eight clock in the morning?" Yesterday was no exception. By the time she turned on the TV and poured her first cup of coffee it was almost 9:30 AM.

The morning copy of the Orange County Register was delivered by 5:30 AM, but that did not matter, as she never went out to fetch it before 10:00 AM. Yesterday she was shocked to see Fred Dupree's paper still on his front step. That was yesterday, today she picked up her paper and stole a glance across the street. She quickly became alarmed as her instincts told her something was wrong. Two papers on the Dupree porch made no sense; even though the California morning temperature was near seventy degrees, she felt a strange shiver go around her shoulders and down her arms.

The Petrillos and Duprees had been neighbors for several years. After Fred's wife died several years ago, he rarely traveled and if he did go out of town, he would always make arrangements for Phillis to pick up his paper. This is very irregular she thought to herself. Setting the paper down in her kitchen, she dialed the Dupree number. After three rings it went to an answering machine. Phillis did not even bother leaving a message—she immediately hung up and dialed 911.

Phillis Petrillo's 911 call was routed to the sheriff's department radio dispatch center. The actual name was the Emergency Communication Bureau.

The dispatcher entered the information into the computer system and at the same time initiated a radio call to Villa Park.

Deputy Erin Heap was patrolling on Taft Street when the welfare check call came in. Canyon Circle was about a minute away and she saw what appeared to be the reporting party as she pulled her sheriff's car up to the address. Heap let dispatch know that she was 10-97, and she then walked over to the woman whom she figured was Mrs. Petrillo.

"Are you Mrs. Petrillo?" asked Deputy Heap.

"Yes, and thank you for coming so fast. Fred never leaves his papers out, and I am concerned that something is wrong. I tried to call but I just got his message machine. I also tried his door and he did not answer."

"Thank you, and if you would just wait on your property, I will have a look around," responded the deputy sheriff.

"Officer, I have Fred's key if you need it."

"Thank you, but let me look around first." And with that, Erin Heap walked up to the front door.

Welfare calls were common and if there were probable cause to think there was an emergency, the deputy knew she could enter the home without a search warrant. After several door knocks and attempts at the doorbell, Sheriff Heap decided to try entry to the backyard. The side yard had a six-foot vinyl solid gate with an unlocked latch. As she entered the backyard, she noticed that the Southern California Edison electrical meter was a little too active for daytime without the air conditioner being on. The back door was a French door with screen and she could see that it opened to a family room or den. Deputy Erin Heap could see that a television was on and also observed several lights on in that room. That was enough probable cause for her, so she returned to the front of the house and approached Mrs. Petrillo. "I would like to use that key and make certain that everything is okay."

"Sir... oh, I'm sorry... Officer, I have it right here."

Because she was going to enter the home, Deputy Heap called dispatch and asked for backup. Within a few minutes, a second sheriff's car was parked on Canyon Circle.

The key worked fine and Deputy Erin Heap, now accompanied by her backup, opened the door to the home of Fred Dupree. The deputy sheriff started to announce "Mr. Dupree, Orange County Sheriff," but the words were never completed. The smell of death is unique, and Heap knew before she saw the body that this was a fatality. That was quickly confirmed by the customary flies that surrounded the two-day-old body.

"I'll call in a 927D and then let's clear the house," she told her partner. Erin called dispatch and asked for another backup, and said they had a one or two-day-old body, possible homicide, and better let Chief Genito know. She and her partner then went room by room to clear the house. Then, stepping carefully over the deceased, both deputies stepped outside to get some fresh air and start the process of securing the property.

Because Deputy Heap was the first officer on the scene of a homicide, she was then designated as "The First Officer." As First Officer her three most important duties were first to make a determination with respect to whether the victim was alive; second, to arrest the person who had committed the homicide; and third, to secure and protect the crime area against contamination.

Deputy Heap then returned to her car and secured a box of barrier tape. Both deputies secured the property with yellow tape labeled "Crime Scene Do Not Cross."

Heap then returned to the front door and documented all of her observations after receiving the radio call.

When a deputy has to work in the area of a ripe body, they will sometimes put a dab of Vicks VapoRub up their nose, while others find that chewing on a cigar can also mask the odor of a ripe body.

Deputy Heap could hear on her radio that Chief Genito had acknowledged the 927D. Radio codes started in the late 1930's and have grown to several different systems and codes. The most common are the ten, eleven, and nine codes. T.V. crime shows usually use the ten codes with 10-4 and 10-20 being used to mean "message received" and "what is your location?" The nine-code system uses 927D to mean "possible dead body."

Chapter 7
Purple Cinnamon Band Practice

FORREST LEFT ANOTHER MESSAGE for his father. Not hearing from his father was not that unusual. For one thing, his dad was not a real fan of his answering machine, or any technology other than his television.

Ever since his mother had died, his relationship with his father had been lukewarm at best. Fred had a real problem with Forrest's decision to become a career drummer. His dad knew that Forrest was very bright and felt that his being a drummer was leaving a lot of his talent on the table. Forrest had tried to explain to his father that there was a lot more to drumming than just bouncing sticks on a drum, but it was all to no avail. His father's answer during any conversation was, "Why don't you get a real job?"

Purple Cinnamon were coming over today to practice a couple of new songs that they were adding to their sets. Forrest had rented a three-bedroom home in Stanton. Not a great area, but the price was right and the bedrooms were big—big enough that he had converted one of them into a music practice room. He had two sets, or kits, of drums, one he left at home, and the other he called his gig kit that he would use for the Cinnamon's gigs. None of this would be possible if his dad did not hate the IRS.

Fred Dupree had been very successful and had accumulated a sizable net worth. It killed him that the IRS would grab a large percentage of his estate when he died, so he gifted his son $10,000 each year to reduce his taxable estate and lower the bill to the god damn IRS. Every December he would give him a check and then say, "Forrest, I do not know what I hate more, the IRS or your drums. Merry Christmas."

Looking out of the kitchen window he saw Shawn Watanabe walking up the driveway, black tennis shoes, and of course the Boston baseball jersey.

Opening the door, Shawn walked directly to the coffee pot, grabbed a Purple Cinnamon coffee cup and sat down at the kitchen table. "Check out that issue of Modern Drummer," says Forrest as he pointed to a stack of music magazines. "Great article on Max and Jay Weinberg. I have no idea how they work for Springsteen and still do the TV gig for Conan."

"That easy, they do not have to coach a baseball team," said guitarist Watanabe. "Forrest, I don't think you read the articles, I think you just look at all the pictures of the new drum gear."

Forrest replied, "Speaking of new gear, I'm thinking of getting a Zildjian 20-inch Oriental China Trash."

Just then Forrest's cell rang, and it was Coyne and Boseman saying that they were five minutes away. "I will get my axe and charts," said Shawn as he returned to his car.

A few minutes later everyone was in Forrest's practice room setting up their gear. Leatha, with help from Leon, brought in her own Roland. Shawn and Leon were able to hook up to the amps that Forrest had in the music room and were ready to rock in just a few minutes.

As the band manager, Forrest got the sheet music, or charts, for the new material. Sheet music, or music tabs, has always been a subject of very opinionated debate with musicians. A band that is going to do studio work or theater will usually be able to read music, or sight-read. Sight-reading is taking a new sheet and being able to play their instrument the first time through. A club or cover band musician can get away with playing by ear. From day one, Forrest made reading music a core value to being a member of Purple Cinnamon. Lucky for him that Shawn was a sight-reader and backed up the rule.

Forrest's studio drum kit was larger then his travel gear. A Mapex Meridian Maple Studioease kit, 7 ply maple, with a 22 X 18 bass, 10 X 8 and 12 X 9 tom toms, 14 X 14 and 16 X 16 floor toms, and a 14 X 5.5 snare are the core set. His various cymbals are all Zildjian. His dream kit would be Ludwig Classic Maple Series with lots of extra floor toms.

After about an hour and a half Shawn said he needed to get to the ballpark. Shaun and Forrest had been friends since Cal State Fullerton. Shaun's signature was his black high top Converse All-Stars, which he wore with black laces and black socks. Others would have argued that his Boston Jersey and ballcap were his trademark. Shaun had traditional Japanese features, as his father who was born in L.A., was of full Japanese ancestry. Shaun's father, a C.P.A., was one of Shaun's coaches during his little league days. Now Shaun was doing the coaching, as the junior varsity coach at El Dorado High School in Placentia California.

"If I don't get going, fifteen sixteen-year-olds are going to be without my leadership," Shaun announced. By now Leon and Leatha were comfortable with the new material. They also needed to get back to their homes because of obligations with their regular jobs.

Leatha and her husband, Mitch Boseman, were both realtors who centered their practice in Orange County. Their real estate business gave Leatha the flexibility to work around Cinnamon's gig schedule. Most of the followers of the band would have agreed that Leatha was the most classy of the band members. She wore her black hair short with a wave over her right forehead. While the guys were dressed in jeans and t-shirts, Leatha would wear a dress with straps that showed just enough cleavage to get attention but not so slutty as to offend anyone.

Everyone packed up and headed out and Forrest's home became unusually quiet.

Chapter 8
Orange County Sheriff's Department, Homicide Detail

"THE GUY IS A fucking pig," muttered Christie under her breath.

"Let me guess, you're pissed again at Simcic," responded Christie's partner Sandy Anderson.

"Sandy, Simcic is the biggest douchebag in the department, and I do not mean the homicide department, I don't mean investigations, I am talking about the whole damn OC Sheriff department."

"Christie, it is not good to hold your feelings inside, express your true feelings," joked Sandy.

"The guy has a neck and head like a bull frog and a gut like a pregnant rhino. If that jerk hits on me one more time I am going to cut off his two-inch dick and then march into the Sheriff's office and put it in her coffee cup."

Detective Christie Cloud had been transferred from gang enforcement four years earlier and was one of the homicide detail's top investigators. Deputy Cloud had been on a fast track since joining the OCSD eight years ago. It seemed like just yesterday that she had been snowboarding through the mountains of Vermont.

A full ride track & field scholarship from the University of Southern California had brought her to Southern California. For three of her four years at USC, Christie's five foot nine inch athletic and slender body threw the 600g Long Tom Turbo Javelin for several Pac 10 records. A serious episode of bursitis and tendonitis of the shoulder ended her track & field career. Academically, Christie was an honor student and graduated with a degree in psychology. Her goal was to be a social worker, but during her senior year, she discovered that most of those desiring to be social workers had more head problems than the people they were supposed to help.

A college friend interviewed for, and was selected to be, a postal inspector for the United States Postal Service. She suggested that Christie look into law enforcement. Christie felt that Los Angeles Sheriff's Department was too large, so she pursued a career with the Orange County Sheriff's Department. Christie took the Law Enforcement Agency Test and breezed through the twenty-eight-week academy. At the age of twenty-two Christie Cloud was sworn in as a Deputy Sheriff. A large percentage of new deputies are first assigned to custody. The department has five different jails that have an average daily inmate population of seven thousand inmates.

It is normal for a new deputy to spend five years as a jailer, and then if they are not proficient their first year of patrol, they will be reassigned back to custody. Deputy Cloud was transferred to gang enforcement after just two years working in the jails, which is very unusual. She did very well with the gang unit and was surprised that she was transferred to the coveted homicide unit.

Christie's thoughts were interrupted by the loud and irritating voice of Sergeant Mike Simcic. "Cloud, today you are going to work for a living—don't screw it up. We got a homicide in Villa Park."

"I'm rolling," said Deputy Christie.

"And guess what, I'm going with you. You drive," added the supervisor of the homicide detail. It was beyond Christie's 155 IQ how Mike Simcic was promoted to Sergeant and worse how he was transferred into homicide.

Sergeant Mike Simcic was a native of Southern California who had played a fair game of football at the small Servite Catholic High School in Orange County. He had been a good enough guard and center that he had received a scholarship to the University of Oregon in Eugene. A knee injury wiped out his senior year, or as Simcic would tell you, "I was going to be a first round N.F.L. draft choice."

An Oregon Duck Alum helped Mike get a job with the Eugene P.D. Eugene had a population of 125,000 and the Eugene P.D. had 180 cops.

Patrolman Simcic stayed with the Eugene Department for six years, and at the age of 28 he moved backed to Southern California.

Mike contacted the OCSD and pulled off a lateral transfer. He applied for a waiver from the California Police Officers Standards Training. Simcic was able to receive a B.C.W., or a basic course waiver, and got his POST certificate. The Central Jail was Mike's first OCSD home for two years, and then he was a jailer at the Theo Lacy facility for eighteen months. After his time with custody duty, Deputy Simcic was selected to be one of twenty-five assigned to Stanton under their service agreement with the O.C. Sheriff Department. Mike worked out of Stanton for almost two years before returning to H.Q. with an assignment with the Special Investigative Bureau, specifically working with the dope team.

It was in narcotics that he was promoted to Sergeant and then within six months he landed in the Homicide Detail and soon had a supervisory role.

As Christie drove to Villa Park, Sergeant Simcic gave her a history lesson on crime in Villa Park. "You know this homicide is going to be high profile," Simcic bantered in his own profound manner. "I think this is only the second killing in VP. An ex-stripper by the name of Janie Pang was living in Villa Park with her kids. I think she was separated from her husband Danny Pang. Danny Pang ran this billion-dollar investment operation that the FBI, and I think the SEC, said was a big Ponzi scheme. About May 1997 a guy in a business suit arrives at Janie's house in VP. The maid opens the door and the suit pulls a gun—chases Mrs. Pang through the house and shoots her. Danny Pang's attorney was named McDonald. He looked like the suit who came to the door. Attorney McDonald drove to San Jose and faked a suicide. The attorney left a note, his watch, and stuff for his wife and pretended to jump off the Golden Gate Bridge. We thought it was fake and stayed on the case for years. In 2001, we got a clue that he was in Salt Lake. There was a long stakeout and our detectives got him. Long trial in 2002, and the jury was deadlocked 10 to 2 in favor of acquittal. Prosecutors decided not to retry the case. This case is going to remind everyone of the Janie Pang murder."

As Investigator Cloud pulled the unmarked sedan up to the crime scene, Sargent Simcic said, "You take the lead, I will hang back and snoop around."

Yellow crime tape was draped all over the front yard and the tape extended to the side yards as well.

Cloud and Simcic saw the three deputy cars and also the unmarked SUV of Chief Genito.

Lt. Vince Genito walked over to Investigator Cloud and Sargent Simcic. Genito said, "Good to see you guys, this is going to be a circus. I am sure the city manager and every city council member will be up my ass in the next thirty minutes. My deputy found the body about forty minutes ago, called it in, cleared the house and did the tape thing. It's all yours. After you get a lay of the land, let me know how we can support Homicide. Looks like a head-shot about two days old, getting ripe."

Chapter 9
Crime Scene

DETECTIVE CLOUD STEPPED OVER the yellow crime tape and walked up to the front door of Fred Dupree's home on Canyon Circle. "Who was the first deputy on the scene?" asked Cloud. Erin Heap told Christie that she had received the call from dispatch. Before she entered the home, Detective Cloud debriefed Deputy Heap on all the situation details including the temperature of the house, what lights were on and the status of the T.V. Christie then walked up to the door, put on a pair of gloves, took a big breath, and entered the home.

Christie had been taught three very important core rules with conducting crime scene investigations. First, respect the scene, keep it clean, minimize contamination, and do not give into pressure to open up the crime scene. The second rule was to start the investigation at fifty thousand feet, and slowly work down to the little details. You didn't want to get all caught up on evidence under the fingernails and not see another body ten feet away. The third core rule was to not jump to conclusions, but to let the accumulation of evidence bring you to a conclusion.

As she stepped into the house, she glanced at the body but resisted focusing just on the victim. Instead, she started by looking at the furniture, lighting and general room configuration. Christie knew she would be calling the OC Crime Lab, but wanted to scope out the situation before placing the call.

The Orange County Crime Lab was one of the best in the country. Investigator Cloud had one hundred percent faith in their forensic abilities. They had over one hundred and fifty people to help with photography, evidence collection, and forensic analyses. The OC Lab had four bureaus and the identification bureau had the forensic scientists and specialists who would work the scene. Christie would make her own notes of possible evidence that she wanted to follow up on with the lab. Her eyes took in three cartridge cases, the status of the home alarm system and the antique chair that was tipped over. She then called dispatch and had them notify the lab.

The floor in the entryway was made of a type of tile or granite and was composed of what appeared to be twelve by twelve tiles. She used this knowledge as she sketched out a floor diagram. The tiles made it easy to add dimensions to her stick figure drawing.

"Did you call for a forensic team yet?" asked Sargent Simcic.

"Yes, they're on their way." replied Christie.

"Neighbor says the house is owned by a widower—the name is Fred Dupree, about seventy, and he has a son who lives in Stanton." continued Simcic.

She noted what Mike had told her and also made a note of a button she saw near the hand of the victim.

Mike Simcic, being very careful with his steps, got up and close to the head wound. "Sure looks like a couple of large caliber, I would be surprised if they turn out to be nine millimeter or thirty eight. Regardless, looks like at least one exited with a good part of his skull and brain. I do not think the autopsy will show that he died from high cholesterol." Christie just shook her head. She had learned it was better to not respond to every comment by the Sergeant or he would go on all day.

She continued to draw her stick figure of the body on the floor and even drew a sketch of the over turned chair. She knew that the forensic team from the OC Crime Lab would photograph and even video the scene and the collection of evidence, but there was always the possibility, though remote, that a camera could malfunction.

"I am going to work the rest of the house. Do want to join me?" she asked the Sergeant.

"I'll step outside for some good air and see if lab is coming."

Christie then located the garage and spent about twenty minutes taking notes as she went through the garage and his car, noting anything that looked out of place in a garage. She then went back into the house and went room to room, also looking in the closets. She noted that an expensive watch was in plain sight in the master bedroom.

The kitchen was clean; dishes all put away, and paper plates in the garbage. The refrigerator was also clean and had the expected minimum food of an elderly widower. The phone answering machine was flashing red. Christie went through eight messages that were left on the machine. Caller ID showed eleven incoming calls. Two of the eight messages were from his son Forrest. She then went back through the caller ID and wrote down his number.

In the den, Cloud found a Waterford Crystal glass that was about a third full of a liquid. A Samsung cell phone lay next to the glass. Christie noted that the battery bar was down to one bar. The log showed that the only activity was a call from his son Forrest twenty-four hours earlier. The thermostat indicated that neither the heat nor air were on. The more accurate the temperature calculations, the more precise would be the estimation of the time of death—however, after twenty-four hours the body core temperature would not be that useful.

When she returned to the front door foyer, she saw the two CSI Specialists from the lab's identification bureau doing P.E.C., that is, photographing and evidence collection. Each hand of the deceased had been secured in plastic gloves to preserve any evidence that could be on the hands or under the fingernails. When it came to evidence collection, you did not try and save trees—a separate container or bag was used for each piece to avoid any cross contamination. The use of forensic science in criminal investigations was a double-edged sword. The good news was that advanced technology could be a tremendous help, and the bad news was that advanced technology had created a new level of expectation, and juries expected T.V.-type CSI work on every case.

"Are you Investigator Cloud?" asked one of the forensic specialists.

"Yes, Christie Cloud."

"I'm Juan Roberto and this is Robert Sanderson. Sergeant Simcic wanted me to tell you that he caught a ride back to the headquarters. Looks like we will be a couple more hours. Did you see anything in the other rooms that you want us to pay special attention to?"

"Yes, picture and grab the glass and cell phone in the den and the answering machine in the kitchen."

Christie returned to the kitchen and captured more of her thoughts and observations on paper. One of her notes was that a wallet belonging to Fred Dupree was in the bedroom and it contained four hundred dollars.

When the specialists finished she would call Simcic and coordinate the notification of next of kin.

Chapter 10
Notification

THE DRIVE TO STANTON was only about twenty to thirty minutes from Santa Ana. Victim notification is by far the most dreaded part of a public safety career. Christie grabbed her partner to accompany her on the notification call.

Detective Cloud and Sandy Anderson had been partners in the homicide unit for about a year. Their partnership came with some productive synergism. Christie was more expressive and outgoing, and Detective Anderson was more subdued and analytical. Her five foot ten inch solid frame was a contrast to Christie's slender five foot nine.

Sandy Anderson paid her OCSD dues with the normal four years in custody, and then she was assigned as an investigator with sex. The Special Victims Detail not only worked with the victims of sexual assaults, but was also involved with the SONAR team. The SONAR program is the sex offender notification and registration team.

Christie drove west on the Garden Grove freeway and discussed the Dupree case with Sandy. What they found puzzling was that it did not appear to be a robbery—there were just too many valuables left in the house. Sandy added her thoughts. "The drug motive does not fly on this case, and the jealous husband also does not fit. Maybe mistaken identity, or was he a witness to a big crime? Christie, I have no clue."

Stanton was located on the west side of Orange County, situated between Anaheim, Cypress and Garden Grove.

Anderson said, "I heard one of the Commanders talking about the Villa Park murder. Said the body was a mess after two days and left a lot of his brains on the floor. He also said it was like the Pang case all over."

"I hope not. Technically the Pang case is unsolved because Danny Pang is dead and the jury was deadlocked for Pangs attorney," replied Christie.

The department had a set procedure for notifications and face-to-face is the preferred method. Because thirteen percent of homicides are committed by family members, Christie wanted to be able to observe the reaction and body language when a next of kin was notified. The thirteen percent figure is much higher when you exclude all of the big city urban homicides. The figure for suburban America is much higher.

"Sandy, the son's name is Forrest Dupree, thirty-two, single, and as far as we know he plays in a rock-n-roll band," commented Christie. A few minutes later she pulled the unmarked up to the curb and both she and Sandy got out. Sandy used her two-way and let dispatch know that they were 10-97 for notification.

Forrest had been in his music room using a drum key to tune the head of one of his floor toms. He went to the kitchen to refill his coffee when he saw two women get out of a sedan that was parked in front of his home. What the hell could they be selling, he thought as they walked up to his door. Forrest pulled open his front door before the two homicide detail investigators could knock.

Christie was the first to speak. While displaying her ID she said "I'm Investigator Christie with the Orange County Sheriff's department and this is my partner Sandy Anderson. Are you Forrest Dupree?"

Forrest's mind was going a hundred miles an hour. What the hell did I do, he thought.

"Yes, I'm Forrest."

"May we come in please?" asked Christie.

Forrest invited them in and everyone continued to stand.

"May we sit down?" asked Christie.

After they were all seated at the kitchen table, Christie said, "Forrest, we are here because of a situation with your father Fred Dupree."

"What happened?" asked Forrest with a voice filled with concern.

"Your father was the victim of a homicide, he was killed in a shooting at his home, a day or so ago, and his death was discovered this morning. We are so sorry to have to bring you this terrible news."

"There has to be a mistake!" exclaimed Forrest. "He is seventy and lives alone in Villa Park. It's impossible."

"Forrest there is no mistake, I was at his home in Villa Park. I am so sorry to have to bring you this news." Christie then asked, "Are you all right? Is there anyone you can call to be with you?"

He did not answer, but said, "Damn, I don't believe it. I was trying to call him all day yesterday. What happened? Was it a robbery or a home invasion? God, I don't believe it—my dad shot."

"Forrest do you want to call anyone?" This time it was Sandy who asked.

"I am sorry," said Forrest, "do you guys want some coffee or water? This is unreal. Yes, I am going to call my best friend."

Shaun Watanabe did not have a baseball game or a practice that afternoon, but he did have a couple of private lessons scheduled. The local high school let him use their batting cages and the thirty dollars for a half hour lesson made his economics work, mostly because the IRS did not get their cut of his income from private lessons.

Shaun's cell's ring tone played *Take me out to the ball game*, and he saw that the call was from Dupree. Five minutes later he had cancelled his lessons and was driving to Forrest's house.

"Forrest, we realize this is a terrible time, but if you are up to it, we would like to ask a couple of questions about your father." asked Investigator Cloud.

Forrest did not answer, but nodded an okay to Christie.

"Can you think of anyone who would want to harm your father?" she questioned. Christie and Sandy continued asking Forest questions about his father for about thirty minutes. There was nothing in Forrest's answers that give them any leads in the case.

"Forrest, we need your help. We have to include family members as suspects until they can be eliminated. As of now we feel that your father was killed in the early evening the day before yesterday, probably between seven and ten. Can you tell us where you were Saturday evening, between seven and ten?" asked Christie.

"Fuck, are you shitting me, we are talking about my dad!" shouted Forrest.

"Forrest, the quicker we can cross off your name, the quicker we can hit the streets and find out who killed your dad—you want us to do that, right?" asked Sandy.

Forrest took a deep breath and re-took control of his emotions, stood up, and said, "Does anyone want some coffee?"

Without waiting for an answer, Forrest got up and made a cup of coffee. Taking his time, he returned to the table and looked both detectives in the eye. "I apologize for getting defensive, but a few minutes ago, you informed me that my father had been shot. I understand your job. I want to make your job easier, not harder. Ladies, Saturday night I was in Yorba Linda between five and midnight. I was with about three hundred people at the Nixon Presidential Library. Our band, Purple Cinnamon, performed at the Boys and Girls Club fundraiser. After I packed up my drum kit, I drove home. I have no alibi between midnight and eight Sunday morning."

Chapter 11
Gentleman's Club

HE KNEW VERY WELL when it had started—call it a compulsion or a fetish, it did not matter—what mattered was that it had controlled a big part of his life for the past thirty-five years. He drove down the Issaquah Fall City Road, passing a Boeing office building. Soon he would be on the I-90 West heading for Lake City and his favorite gentleman's club. Hal was eighteen, maybe nineteen, when his life changed and he became a slave to his addiction.

Playing football in his friend Bobby's backyard had been a daily activity during the summer evenings. Hal had always been a natural when it came to athletics, and he had been especially talented at football. His friend had gone into his house for something and Hal had been just killing time in the backyard. Because it was dusk, he had noticed when a basement light in Bobby's house had gone on. The window and window well had been located at ground level. Thinking that it was his friend, Hal had crawled over to the window and peeked in. The window had looked into a basement bathroom and shower.

Hal Ruhall, successful business executive, turned his 760Li BMW onto I-90 West. Just remembering that evening, over thirty years ago, caused him to have an enormous hard-on. She was Bobby's aunt, his mother's sister. At that age you never knew or cared how old somebody was. All he knew was that those five minutes of voyeurism were the most erotic five minutes of his life. Five minutes that he would relive and relive over a thousand times. Five minutes that dominated his sexual preferences for the rest of his life.

Even though the window was rain-spotted and a little dirty, Hal had had a clear view of the shower and his friend's aunt. To this day he could not remember if she had been a large women, all he remembered was that she was in the shower and that she had had the most enormous breasts an eighteen year old could imagine.

Hal forced himself back to reality just long enough to check his BMW's speed and adjust his crotch to make his huge erection more comfortable.

She would lift up each one of her extremely big tits and rub them with soap. She had a soap bar in one hand and would run the bar under and then over the top of each one. After the thorough soaping of each breast, she turned slightly to return the soap bar to its little alcove in the side of the shower. As she adjusted the showerhead, Bobby's Aunt glanced up at the window that he was staring through.

It appeared that she had seen him but she had made no sudden movements or reaction to confirm that he was caught. Instead she reached for a bottle of shampoo and squirted a large portion of the liquid into her hand. She then lifted up each of those most beautiful breasts and proceeded to rub the shampoo over and over her erect and large nipples. As she did this to first one then the other breast she had turned so that she was facing directly toward the window and his new sexual appetite. To this day Hal could remember every detail of those huge breasts. This trip to Seattle and the gentleman's club would be one of many such trips to relive those five minutes so many years ago.

The BMW drove past one, then another, of Seattle's tittie bars. Déjà vu, Show Girls, Lusty Lady and Rick's were some of the more well-known topless establishments. As usual, Hal drove passed those clubs and went directly to the parking lot of The Lotus Girl Gentleman's Club. Hal was no stranger to the Lotus Girl, but there he was known only as Frankel. No last name, just Frankel.

Chapter 12
Forrest's Home

"I THINK I'M A damn suspect," said Forrest, as Shawn took a seat in the family room, or what used to be called a TV room. A sofa, two Lazy Boy recliners and a sixty-inch flat screen filled up the room. Shawn had arrived about fifteen minutes after the OCSD detective had left.

"Forrest, that is just routine stuff, they aren't serious—they always do that on the TV cop shows."

"But the problem Shawn, is I was here all night. I do not have an alibi," said Forrest as he rubbed his head.

"Did you make any cell calls while you were here that would show on your call log and maybe that would prove you were here?" Shawn questioned.

"I drop my cell on the counter when I walk in the door and pick it up when I leave," Forrest said.

"Forrest, you know I watch a lot of the crime shows, you know, *Law and Order*, *CSI* and stuff; they always say that to be a suspect, you need to have a motive *and* you have to have opportunity. What is your motive? We are talking about your father." Shawn argued.

"Friend, my father was very wealthy, just the house is a million. I will inherit millions. I could get three, maybe four million, I am the only child, and I don't think he was much into charity." Forrest said in a low voice. "The cop said that his house is still a crime scene and is still off limits. She thought I could enter the home late tomorrow or the next day. I don't want to go there," said Forrest.

"We will go together," replied Shawn. "Forrest, you need to call Leon and Leatha," he added.

The TV was on but nobody was watching it. Leon had picked up a bottle of Patron, and Leatha was sipping wine from a bottle of Napa Cabernet that she was saving for the weekend. Forrest was half-listening to his band members, as his mind kept drifting back to his father.

His relationship with his father had been pretty good until about three years ago. When his dad had been running Dupree Environmental Solutions he had not had time to worry about Forrest and his misguided career. It was only after his mom had died three years earlier that he had started to grind on him about getting a real job. They did not scream and yell at each other, but they would argue at least once a week about his Dad's engineering degree and how hard he had worked to build his company from scratch. These thoughts made Forrest feel guilty, and he tried to remember his last conversation with his father.

Shawn's voice brought him back to reality. "What do you want to do with our next few gigs?" Shawn asked.

"We have tomorrow, Saturday and a mid-week gig on Wednesday," replied Forrest. And he added, "I want to do them, I want to stay busy. Unless that cop lady arrests me. This shit is unreal. I will say, the one called Christy is really foxy. She is about five eight or nine, good looking dark hair and the best part is she's got a gun."

Half an hour later, the Purple Cinnamon members had gone home, and all of a sudden Forrest's home had become very quiet. He left the TV on, and went directly to the music room and picked up his sticks, more specifically his Pro Mark Hickory 720 Intruders. These sixteen and a half inch sticks were perfect for his large hands. Is this a dream or what, he thought, as he tried to release his frustration out on his drum kit. An hour later he threw his sticks against the wall, just missing a poster of Rush, and headed to bed.

Chapter 13
Homicide detail

THE HOMICIDE DETAIL WAS very quiet at six forty-five am when Detective Cloud arrived. Christie tried to get a jump on the day and was usually one of the first to hit the office.

The sheriff headquarters were located in a congested part of Santa Ana, a little west of I-5 and south of the 22 freeway. 550 N. Flower Street was the home of the majority of the OCSD, with the exception of the crime lab, communications, and custody operations, often referred to as the jails. Located next to headquarters, the central jail complex housed over 2,600 inmates. Other sheriff jails were the Musick and Theo Lacy facilities, with another 4,200 plus guests.

The office space of the homicide detail was up on the second floor of the department's three floors, and Christie's workstation was as far away from Sergeant Simcic as possible. She thought about the conversation she had had with Sandy Anderson as they returned from the next of kin notification. Most important, they had both agreed that Forrest Dupree was good looking and were surprised that he was still single. Christie made sure that Sandy knew that she had first dibs on Forrest because it was her case.

While Christie told Forrest Dupree about the death of his father, Sandy was able to observe his body language and his neuro-linguistic behavior and felt certain that his reaction profile was in line with a person receiving news that a parent had been killed. The problem thought Christie was his lack of an alibi, but maybe the case would get a break when the forensics came in.

"Cloud, do you have a person of interest yet?" shouted Mike Simcic from across the department.

"Not yet, Sergeant," replied Christie as she rolled her eyes.

"Well, check this out. Looks like your boy Forrest is now a wealthy drummer. His old man was worth over a million," said the homicide detail supervisor, as he handed Christie a draft of a real-estate extract of the deceased's home. "No mortgage. That will buy the kid a lot of new drums."

Christie has been working with Simcic for three of the last four years that she had been assigned to homicide and he had been her supervisor for two and a half years. It is not just his irritating personality that grated on her, but her boss was physically repulsive. Maybe it started with his five foot seven inch height and his two hundred plus weight. Simcic said he was a football player in college and was always bragging about an overdeveloped chest and inflated biceps. Then there was his very fat neck and a face that always had that stupid grin. How can a guy so ugly think he is so sexy, she wondered.

Each investigator had their own six by six foot Herman Miller modular workstation, and Christie had corkboard on two of the three panels. She was the master of lists and her most important list was pinned in the center of her workstation. Her key list was a series of questions that she needed answers to on the Dupree homicide. How did the perp get into the house? Why were there three cartridge cases when it looked to her and Mike like the vic received two head shots? If they excluded son Forrest, what was the motive? There was no robbery. Christie looked at those questions and several more. The autopsy would be performed that afternoon and she told Sergeant Simcic that she would be there.

Before she released, or opened, up the crime scene, she needed to go back to the house and try and get more answers. Once the scene was released there would be instant contamination, and the crime scene would be worthless for further investigation.

"Sandy, I want to go back to Villa Park for another couple of hours," Christie said. "Grab a couple of those empty file boxes."

It only took them fifteen minutes to pull up to the Dupree house on Canyon Circle. The yellow crime tape was still circling the property. Using her cell phone, she called the office of Lt. Vince Genito. "Chief this is Cloud from homicide. I am back at the Dupree house for more investigation if you want to stop by and compare notes."

Genito replied, "Good idea, I would like to get out of this office, the local heat is on—be up there in a few minutes."

They unlocked the door and walked around the plastic that covered the floor where the victim had been shot. Most of the odor had dissipated. The chair was still on its side and half-covered by the plastic.

"If we knew what we were looking for, we would have solved the case." Christie told Sandy. She added, "The key word is motive. Why would anyone want to kill Dupree? We will figure out the who later; start in the kitchen and I will take the den."

Investigator Cloud walked to the den and noticed that the drinking glass and cell phone had been bagged and tagged by forensic the team. What could make someone want to kill a seventy-two-year-old retired widower, she wondered half out loud.

The room had a large bookcase but there were very few books. Most of the shelves were filled with family pictures and a few business and professional awards. Next to the bookcase, she saw a two-drawer file cabinet. She pulled open the top drawer and looked at the file tabs. It was obvious that Fred Dupree was an engineer, or he had somebody very analytical organize his files, she thought. It appeared that most of the top drawer dealt with the sale of Dupree Environmental Solutions.

She pulled out a file folder labeled Purchase Agreement and Memorandum of Understanding that was dated September four years earlier. That meant that he sold his business about the time that his wife came down with cancer, she thought, as she looked backup at the row of family pictures. Just then she heard the voice of Lt. Vince Genito.

"Hi there," he announced as he walked through the door of the den.

"Chief, I have about two hours before I need to join the autopsy. I sure hope something shows up. I was going to look through his business files and see if I can spot anything," she said.

"How can I help? The city council is going ballistic over this case, everyone is worried we will have another Pang." Genito volunteered.

"Lieutenant, here are a couple of files on the vic's business that he sold four years ago. I will look through the next drawer."

Both Homicide Investigator Cloud and Villa Park Chief Genito spent the next thirty minutes going over the contents of Fred Dupree's business files.

"My god, Christie, take a look at this."
"Shit, I don't believe it," reacted Cloud.
Vince Genito then said, "I would recommend you call Simcic."

Chapter 14
Evidence

INVESTIGATOR CLOUD CHECKED IN with dispatch and told them that she was out of service. She figured she had enough time to drop by headquarters before she needed to be at the Dupree autopsy, but then she had no desire to see Simcic. Christie needed to tell jerk-face Simcic what she and Lt Genito had discovered in the files of the deceased.

It appeared that between the value of the home, bank accounts, brokerage accounts and future payments from the sale of Dupree's business, he was worth over six million. Simcic would make the big leap and assume that the kid was guilty, because six million was plenty of probable cause.

As she headed toward Flower Street she started to dread the confrontation. She knew she had never been one to avoid conflict, but today Christie was just not in the mood to deal with Mike. A text message to her supervisor would have to do and then she would have to deal with him after she finished observing the autopsy. Parking was always a hassle in Santa Ana, so Christie drove to her usual parking area at the Sheriff's department, and typed a text message to Mike Simcic.

"… Sergeant, Lt. Genito and I found financial info on the vic. Dupree sold his business a couple of years ago and it looks like his net worth could be 6 million or more. Will review details after autopsy…" she hit the send button on her Blackberry and got out of her car.

Investigator Cloud locked her case file in the trunk and started walking down Flower Street. The walk was about three blocks and was just long enough to give her time to clear her head and be in a good mind set for the forensic pathologist. As Christie turns on Santa Ana Blvd, she caught a glimpse of Santa Ana Stadium. It was only eight years ago that she was at USC on a track and field scholarship. She looked at the stadium and flashed back to her days as a javelin thrower. Fifty-three or fifty-four meters was a good throw of her six hundred G turbo javelin. She still had three of the six hundred gram long toms in her Placentia apartment. "I wonder if the javelin could be considered a weapon of mass destruction?" she pondered.

One block to go as she continued down Santa Ana Blvd. Christie looked forward to the autopsy. Most cops didn't like attending an autopsy, not just because of the grossness of the event, but also because it ate up one or two hours in a day that already had too few hours. She had observed her first autopsy three years earlier when she had attended module A and B of the Basic Death Investigation Course. The course was two one-week classes taken at the coroner facility.

The time spent observing autopsies had been interesting for Christie. An autopsy reminded her of watching surgery on the *Gray's Anatomy* TV show. The surgeons did their job, but told jokes and were casual about the work that they did. It did not mean that the surgeons were not professional; it just meant that their casual demeanor kept them relaxed. The same was true with the forensic pathologists. The medical examiners would discuss the previous night's ball game while they removed internal organs and placed them on the pathology scale.

The California Coroners Training Center was a state of the art facility that served a dual role. Many cities and counties used the facility to provide training for their coroners, and also the examination rooms were used by Orange County to perform all of their autopsies. Christie remembered when the fifty thousand square foot building had been completed. The autopsy center was a dream of former Sheriff and Coroner Mike Corona. Too bad Sheriff Corona had had to cool his heels for several years in prison because of a conviction for one count of witness tampering.

It seemed that during Christie's eight years with the department there had been nothing but drama. In addition to Sheriff Corona's trial and conviction, the Orange County Jail was slammed with a big scandal with the death of inmate John Chamberlain. Christie had already moved from lock up to the gang unit, but knew many of the deputies who were investigated after Chamberlain's death.

Chamberlain had been booked for a misdemeanor charge of child porn. Several inmates were convicted of beating the inmate to death because they believed he was a child molester. After a big investigation, the Orange County Grand Jury made fourteen recommendations that included prohibiting watching television and movies while on duty in any of the five jail facilities. The good news was that Christie had already moved to gang and stayed away from the circus.

As she opened the doors to the coroner center, she wondered if the autopsy would answer some of her questions about this case, and secretly she hoped it would get the victim's son off the radar as Simcic's prime suspect. Her big question was about the three shell casings found at the scene and what appeared to be two head wounds on the vic. Two of the casings were .45 calibers and one was a .357 magnum. Real weird, if there were two shooters, then where did the third shot go, and why would there be a .357 casing left behind? Most .357's are revolvers, and revolvers do not eject spent casings like a semi-auto does.

Christie hoped that the lab would soon be finished with their report on the crime scene evidence. She looked forward to their thoughts on the found button, tissue and casings.

Chapter 15
Orange County Medical Examiner

"Detective Cloud to observe the Dupree autopsy," she told the admin staff at the front desk.

"That exam will be conducted by Dr. Romanski in Room Two. You have been here before, right?" was the reply from the career county employee. Christy figured she was in her mid fifties and probably could tell some great stories about what she had seen and heard working for the county coroner.

Before the new facility was built, you had to put your personal equipment in a locker and put on protective clothing. It was also a good idea to put some Vicks in your nose.

Now an autopsy observer would go to an observation room that had a large observation window that looked directly at the stainless steel table for the specific case. A speaker system connected the observer with the Medical Examiner and there was a computer console that let the observer zoom in for a close-up of the examination any time they wanted more detail.

"How involved do you want to be?" hollered Dr. Romanski through the speaker system. "Welcome to Autopsy 101, I am Stan Romanski, but everyone calls me Dr. Ski. Mary Wallace will be my assistant for this case."

"Doctor, I am Detective Christy Cloud, lead on this Dupree case.

This is my second observation, not counting a few I saw completing the basic death investigation course."

Dr. Romanski had been employed by the group of doctors who had had the contract with the county for the last four years. It was not unusual to spend twelve or thirteen years of training before a doctor was board certified. Christy observed that the Doctor was about forty-five, over six feet tall and much too skinny for her liking. He had goggles for eye protection while Mary, the assistant had a full shields for face protection.

"Detective, before I arrived Mary did the X-ray while the body was still bagged and then used our scanning election microscopy on the head because it is a head shot case. I will review the X-rays and S.E.M report after we finish the internal exam. Suffice it to say, stippling, soot and GSR show one entrance wound, appears to show a muzzle to victim distance of intermediate; or in cop speak, the gunshot residue study says one bullet was fired from two to three feet. The labs got his clothes yesterday and they will probably use a Modified Griess Test on his shirt, you guys can compare any nitrite patterns with our S.E.M report," the Doctor contributed.

Christy had good knowledge of the Griess test and the other test, the Sodium Rhodizonate Test. She also knew that forensic science was being challenged because of the green movement. More and more bullets were being manufactured without lead and the S.R.T. was a test that identified the lead in a gunshot pattern and was valuable in determining the distance from a muzzle to the victim.

The assistant had already removed the victim from the white plastic body bag and he was placed face up on the stainless steel exam table. Blue cloth towels covered Fred Dupree's head and waist. An indent tag was tied to his left toe.

Mary held a clipboard and was making notes while Dr. Romanski conducted a visual examination of the body.

"Understand that our friend here was found between twenty-four to forty-eight hours after his death. In that case we will be dealing with both putrefaction and autolysis. Autolysis is where the enzymes in the cells start a process of self-digestion. Bacteria in the intestinal track are slowly released into the body in the process of putrefaction. The mild blotting tells me we are closer to two days then one," said the doctor.

The Medical Examiner then removed the towel from the face and started his visual examination of the face and head. "Detective,

I know you are eager for a cause of death, but I stay with my system and try not to deviate from the process. If I don't stay with the process, I will get eaten alive in court. From my exterior examination of the head it appears we have two maybe three large caliber wounds into and probably through the skull. We will get a better picture when we examine the inside of the skull."

Dr. Romanski alternated talking to Christy, his assistant Mary, and the microphone suspended over the table. Mary replaced the cloth over Dupree's head and face prepared to make the customary Y incision. Mary then took a scalpel and started above the armpit and cut to the top of the sternum and then straight down to the pubic bone. The assistant then cut the subcutaneous fat and muscle in the upper chest and created a triangular flap that exposed the organs in the neck. Over the next fifteen minutes Assistant Wallace and Medical Examiner Romanski started with the diaphragm muscles and exposed the peritoneum cavity, and then cut the ribs and reflected back the chest plate to expose the lungs and heart.

Dr. Ski and Mary continued working up all the organs, especially lungs, heart, liver and spleen. They then put a clamp on the top of the small intestine and removed it in one piece even though it was very blotted. The renal capsules containing the kidneys were removed and labeled and set aside on the dissection board against the wall.

While all this work was being completed, Christy allowed her mind to wander to an evaluation of her internal instincts. Even though Forrest Dupree was the prime suspect in the eyes of Simcic, her gut feeling told her otherwise. No damn way he killed his dad. What complicated this case was that she felt that maybe she had a little crush on Forrest the drummer.

Her daydreaming was interrupted by Romanski as he asked, "Christy, do you know how you can tell the right lung from the left lung? The right lung has three lobes while the left lung has two," he answered before she could answer.

"Interesting. Doctor, anything unusual so far with this autopsy?"

"No, so far, a healthy non-smoking male in his seventies."

"Detective, you have been patient, We will work up the skull and brain next."

The Medical Examiner himself used his scalpel to dissect down and around the neck to remove the neck organs and tongue. He reflected the front of the scalp and the posterior portion so as to expose the skull. "Are you doing okay?" the M.E. asked.

"So far so good."

The doctor continued, "We find that the more senses that are impacted the more likely a person might get sick. First you have the visual, and of course the smell, when we add the saw noise, we find a lot of visitors will get squishy."

"Doctor, I think I am fine, but thanks." she said as she snuck a glance at another table where another M.E. was about to start a autopsy in front of observation room three.

After making the saw cuts, Dr. Ski explained his next steps. "First we need to separate the skull from the dura, that will expose the brain. I just reached down and cut the optic nerves and the other cranial nerves. I just cut the membrane that holds the cerebellum to the base of the skull." He handed the brain to Mary who carried it over to the scale. "We know we have fractures and holes here, but by peeling away the dura matter we will be able observe all the skull fractures."

"It is clear that we have a entrance above the left eye and a exit right here," said the doctor as he showed Christy a jagged hole the size of a silver dollar. "This appears to have been shot at a angle that indicates the shooter was below the victim—or we also see this angle when a victim is shot while prone such as on a bed or couch. The S.E.M. report did not have any noted G.S.R. so we think it was from a distance of more than five feet."

"What about caliber?" asked Christie.

"No 22, 9 or even 38; I put my analysis with 357, 40 or 45mm. The same for the other wound." he added. "Let's look at this other one. Entrance above and front of left ear and exit behind right ear. This track made a real mess of his brain. As I said, Mary's test earlier indicates the gun was two, maybe three feet from the head. Let's go over and take a peek at what is left of the brain. I won't put you through med school with brain lobe 101, but eighty five percent of the brain is the cerebellum and between the two ballistic tunnels it appears that a lot of our vic's frontal lobe and cerebellum are back at the crime scene. We will dissect all the organs and send out the fluid samples for testing. You can stay if you want." said Dr. Ski.

"I need to catch the Sergeant so I will skip out early, but what is your unofficial guess as to how this came down?" Christy asked.

"The perp was standing and the vic was on floor for the first shot.

With the large caliber he would have died instantly. Then the perp gets close and fires the second shot. The S.E.M showed a tight G.S.R. pattern, maybe a suppressor was used," added the doctor. "Mary do you want to add anything?"

"I go with you, Dr. Ski" Mary answered.

As Christy checked out with the front desk she was mentally reviewing the autopsy results she had just observed. As she walked back to the office, she hoped that the fat man with the stupid grin had already left the office. Was it possible that Simcic had received one too many concussions while playing football, she wondered to herself.

Chapter 16
Ecstasy

PACO TINSON PULLED OUT of the Parks and Rec building and turned down Bullis Road. The actual name of his employer was The City of Lynnwood Recreation and Community Services Department. Paco's job at the City of Lynwood was the perfect cover for a gangbanger, drug dealer and hired killer. Paco Tinson was not born a killer, but it became part of his career transition.

Paco was raised by a single mother and had spent his entire life living in the City of Lynnwood. He held no bitterness toward his father who had knocked up his mother while she was a stripper in Los Angeles. Even though he did not stick around after his fling with his mother; he did send money and supported Paco and his mom.

During his last two years at Lynnwood High, Paco formed the FTC Gang. They kept their numbers about twenty and the distribution of ecstasy, or the official name MDMA, was the gang's main criminal enterprise. FTC stood for "Fuck The Cops" and was Paco's real family.

Paco Tinson may have been a twenty six year old drug dealer, but he approached the FTC brothers and X dealing as a business. Paco lived by his rule of three. He demanded that all members of the FTC gang followed his rule of three. Rule one: loyalty to FTC gang. Rule two: sell but never, never use. Rule three: hide the money—no bling, show cars or pimp clothes. His arrest and prosecution record was moderate with his worst conviction a five-year-old class C felony assault case. He had had other bullshit, but nothing for two years when he got a possession with intent to distribute dismissed for lack of evidence. The evidence just disappeared before an Orange County trial.

"This is going to be a busy week," he thought as his tic caused his head to jerk. He had another contract job in Orange County and also needed to orchestrate a pickup of a shipment of ecstasy coming in from Belgium. The key to picking up an MDMA shipment was to break up ten thousand pills as fast as possible so that none of the FTC members were in possession of more than two hundred and fifty pills, or units.

The U.S. sentencing guidelines for possession were a moving target. There were big swings in the amount of jail time for possession and the number was always changing because of court challenges and rule changes. The game was to split the package up over and over until each member was carrying a low number of pills. The pills from Belgium were about thirty-five percent pure. Each three-hundred-milligram tablet might be one hundred twenty-five milligrams of ecstasy and the rest ephedrine and/or caffeine.

Paco pulled his Ford Explorer into a strip mall on Long Beach Blvd. and called his Executive VP. Most gangs used lieutenants and captains like the cops and military, but Paco liked to use business models. "Rodney this is Frances, we have work tomorrow night and I want to coordinate the team with you tonight. Come to my home in about an hour and pick me up a can of carb spray"

He always used phony names when calling his FTC bangers, as they knew his voice and he only used dump phones or burn phones when on a job. Paco pulled back onto Long Beach Blvd. and drove to his private mailbox. He kept a private box for only three months and then he would close the account and open up another. The key to the box was hidden in the back of his Ford. If he was picked up, he did not want the key to his private box on his car key ring.

Inside the mailbox was the package he was expecting. He closed the box and walked past his car and headed to the nearby McDonald's. He ordered some nuggets and a coke set them down on a table that appeared to be away from most of the other customers. Paco then walked into the restroom. A stall was open, so he entered carrying the package concealed under his light jacket.

Once inside the stall, he opened up the thick shipping package, one of those that you would use to ship a book or DVD. He pulled the tab, and was quickly thumbing through the forty thousand in one hundreds. He ripped off the address label, and after tearing it into small pieces he flushed it down the toilet. Before he left the restroom he threw the rest of the wrappings in the garbage. Also included in the bundle of money was a three by five card with a name and address printed on it: *Harvey A Flag / Laguna Woods.*

Fuck, he thought as he headed to his Ford with four hundred Franklins stuffed in his jacket. Twenty thousand were for the completion of the hit on Dupree in Villa Park and twenty thousand were for this week's hit on Flag in Laguna Woods. What upset him were two hits in just a few days in the same county. The pick and split from Belgium was not going to be too much heavy lifting but he would need to spend a bunch of hours setting up the Laguna Woods hit.

Paco went to his door to let one of the FTC boys in. Jose threw the can of carburetor cleaner at Paco and asked, "What are you going to do with carb spray?"

"Let me share one of the secrets of the universe. This shit will do anything. Just like WD-40, it will do a hundred things. Jose, one can of carb will kill ants, wasps, clean your engine and just like pepper spray it will blind your opponent for a good half hour".

"Paco, where do come up with this shit?" Jose asked.

Changing the subject, Paco discussed the Belgium shipment and the needed precautions that FTC must take. "We got ten thousand X's coming in tomorrow and I want the shit split real fast. If our guys get caught with two hundred they will probably do no time, if we don't split the load fast and they get caught with eight hundred or a thousand units, we will lose them for five years. We got to receive and split the load super fast. Are we cool?"

"Yes boss", Jose said as he headed out of Paco's apartment.

Paco then settled down to several hours of research for the week's hit on Harvey A. Flag of Laguna Woods. He used a fifteen-inch Mac Pro and did all his searches using the search engine ixguick. The cops could get all his search history from Google, but ixquick was based in the Netherlands and did not record its users' IP addresses.

What should have taken Paco three or four hours to research was inevitably going to take him six or even eight hours. It was not his muscle twitch or tick that was going to slow him down, but his brain dust that was going to jump into his brain and send his mind on a crazy journey.

He was using Google Satellite to look over the roads and neighborhoods in Laguna Woods when he decided to check the phase of the moon. Satisfied that there was not going to be a full moon tomorrow, he then allowed his brain dust to let his focus shift over the power of the moon, tides and lunacy. An hour had passed and he had gone from the metamorphic changes in a werewolf to the influences of lunacy on the Salem Witches.

Before turning off his MacBook, he opened up an application called "Scanner H.D." He monitored the Los Angeles P.D. and L.A. Sheriff department and listened for any radio traffic that would signal trouble for the shipment of ecstasy that had come in that night.

Chapter 17
Poor Man's Pepper Spray

WHILE DRIVING EAST ON the 91 freeway, Paco reviewed the zillion things he had accomplished in the last forty-eight hours. His gang buddies had picked and split the Belgium MDMA, the process of getting out of LAX had gone flawlessly, and the gang members each had between five hundred and a thousand X tablets that would be sold at a street price of about ten dollars a tablet. Fifteen years ago, X was going for thirty-five dollars per tablet. It was a concern that the gross price of a unit was down sixty percent and the jail sentencing guidelines had more than doubled.

He had one of the brothers locate a clean nine-millimeter Taurus PT 92. The Taurus was just as good as the highly touted Beretta 92. Even though Flag's house was on a large lot and at the end of a cul-de-sac, he was a little concerned about noise. He had loaded the Taurus with one-hundred-forty-seven grain Hydra-Shok. Using the heavy bullet would make the rounds subsonic and substantially reduce the noise.

When a bullet has a smaller size, for example the typical one-hundred-fifteen grain, it will go supersonic and make a load crack, or report sound. He hoped the subsonic load would not alert the neighborhood. As an added precaution, he asked that the PT 92 be adapted for a can. A can is a suppressor, and in this case, Paco had a Ti-Rant suppressor made by AAC.

Paco kept his eye on his speed as he approached the transition to the 22 East. He took an exit off the freeway and pulled into a side street strip mall, where he took out his cell phone, removed the battery, and pulled out the SIM card. He knew that that was a bit of overkill, but there was no reason to have the technology do a GPS or cell tower trace of his whereabouts. A glance at the dashboard clock intimated that in just forty-five minutes he would be forty thousand dollars richer and Harvey A. Flag would be bleeding out. One more victory for the bad guys.

There was a reason that crime was a non-issue in Laguna Woods, thought Paco Tinson. He read that there was less than one crime per year for every one hundred residences. Doing a hit in Laguna Woods was like breaking into the Philadelphia Mint. There were gates, many with guards, all over the city. Paco knew his strengths and he also knew his weaknesses. He was good at planning and he had put in nearly eight hours going over this hit. He was certain that he had covered all the speed bumps on this hit. Not only had Paco parked his car at a mall up the I-5, but also he had jacked a Honda on the other side of the mall by the Nordstrom store. He put on a dumb looking mustache and a pair of Elvis sunglasses.

Dust was his only weakness, those crazy thoughts that always popped into his mind. He knew he was smart, even figured he had a high IQ, yet he always had to fight dust. His dust tonight was his thoughts about headlights. As he drove south on the 5 freeway, he kept thinking about the different kind of headlights that all the cars had. He needed to focus on his checklist, preparation, staging, the hit, escape and evidence distraction. But he found that he was worried about halogen, Xenon, and pencil beams: dust that caused him to get off focus.

Just before El Toro Road, he pulled off of the I-5 on Paseo De Valencia, a street that should not have had a guard gate. His target house was nearby, so Paco decided to park his stolen car at the St. George's Episcopal Church. His travel bag was on the passenger side floorboard. He was wearing gloves so he was not concerned about fingerprints. He had placed a plastic bag over the headrest to minimize residual DNA from hair or epithelial cells. He grabbed his bag and removed his gloves and also removed the headrest plastic. If the car was recovered before he returned he would have no connection.

His walk was about three blocks and at nine in the evening he did not have a fear of being seen.

The day before, he had developed a way that he could approach the back of the house and gain entry by kicking in a French door. The corner off the house provided a spot to hide his bag and do the staging for this hit.

The gun already had the suppressor attached and the can of carburetor spray he put in his back pocket. A plastic bag was also in his bag and that he put in his jacket pocket. A roll of duct tape he slipped up his arm.

Leaving the bag in the garden he approach the back of the house and the French doors. It appeared that a TV was on in a room next to the kitchen; nobody was visible as he looked into the home. Paco set the carb spray and gun down and placed strips of duct tape over the glass near the lock. A flowerpot was near the porch and he used that to pop the glass of the door. The tape kept the glass from blowing out into the room, yet it still made a lot of noise.

The killer reached through the fracture in the glass and located the deadbolt and opened the door. He now had the carb spray in one hand and held the gun behind his back. Paco Tinson was five feet in the kitchen when Harvey Flag came around the corner yelling, "What's going on? Carol, call 911!" That was the last thing out of Mr. Flag's mouth before a thousand needles of excruciating pain hit his eyes and dropped him to his knees in front of the kitchen stove. The stream of carburetor spray had traveled over ten feet and disabled Harvey Flag in two seconds. Tinson stepped passed his target and was in the Flags' TV room before Mrs. Flag could reach for a phone. Just as Tinson raised his gun for a headshot, a brown haired cocker spaniel came charging into the room. By now Carol Flag was screaming and trying to get out of her chair. Between Harvey's screams of pain, the barking of the small dog, and Mrs. Flags yelling, Paco turned to see what was on their TV. He quickly regained his focus and without letting up on the button, he shot a steady stream of carb spay first at the dog and then into the face of Mrs. Flag and back to the dog. He threw the spray can at the dog and with two hands put two nine-millimeter bullets in the head of Carol Flag. The dog was still howling and was now running around in circles.

He left the dog and quickly returned to the kitchen where he found Mr. Flag trying to get up from the kitchen floor. Paco closed within three of four feet and then delivered a double tap into the back of the head of Harvey A Flag.

Paco Tinson had done his share of killing, his first was another gang banger when he was only eighteen, but he had never killed a dog. If he left the dog it would escape out the broken backdoor. He could lock the dog on the den with the other body but he worried about how long and how loud the dog would bark after his escape. He was not sure if he could hit the small head of the dog so he returned to the den and shot the dog twice in the chest. The dog continued to yelp for one or two seconds then appeared to die.

Paco felt that he had been in the house for an hour but the reality was that everything had taken place in thirty to forty seconds. He took a deep breath and tried to bring his heart rate and breathing back to a normal level. Before leaving the TV room or den he found and pocketed the carb spray. Taking a little more time to locate all six of the 9mm cartridges, he felt he was now in total control of this hit.

Before he left, he felt he had to play with the minds of the crime lab rats. He pulled the plastic bag from his pocket and emptied the contents on the floor in front of the refrigerator. Two old coke cups and two empty French fry bags from McDonald's should keep the cops spinning. What else could he do? He knew he needed to get out of there but this was a game and he could not resist. Tinson stepped around the body of Mr. Flag and opened several cupboards until he located a stack of soup cans. He removed five cans of assorted soups and arranged them in a circle on the floor about eighteen inches from the pool of blood that had formed around Harvey's head.

Tinson removed the warm silencer from the gun, turned off as many lights as he could see and then left after closing the back French doors.

Hope I don't have bad dreams about shooting that little dog, he thought as he put the suppressor, gun, and carb spray back in his bag.

Chapter 18
Purple Cinnamon Practice

The members of Purple Cinnamon had arrived for a band practice at Forrest's home in Stanton. At six o'clock in the evening, there was still an hour of daylight before sunset, and the temperature was above seventy degrees. Two days earlier, the band had been informed that Forrest's father had been killed. Instead of meeting in the band room Forrest had asked the members of P.C. to join him in his den. Forrest sat on a bar stool, while Shaun and Leon shared the couch. There were two armchairs open but Leatha found a spot near the flat screen and remained standing.

Before starting the meeting, Forrest asked the group if anyone needed any beverage or snacks. "Guys, it is natural for there to be some tension in the room. You are not sure what to say or how to say it. First, I am okay, still in a little shock but okay. I cannot change what happened to my dad, but truth being told, I sure as hell would like to know why he was killed. Feel free to ask me any question or discuss what is happening with the police, it does not bother me. Are we cool on that?

"Before we go upstairs and make beautiful music, I would like to ask for a couple of favors. Shawn, would you do me a favor? Next week, Tuesday or Wednesday, I need to go over to my dad's house."

"You want us to join you?" Shawn jumped in.

"No, but thank you," Forrest added. "But I would like someone to go look the house over and let me know what it looks like. I think I want and need to be along for the first time over there, but I do not want to be caught off guard if it is a mess. Shawn, you know what I mean?"

"I will be in Placentia tomorrow. I will drop down to Villa Park after baseball," Shawn volunteered.

"Great, I understand yesterday that they did an autopsy on my dad. This morning I had my dad moved over to the funeral home. I am still thinking about what I might do for a service.

"I spoke to the detective today and it seems to me that they are no closer to who shot my dad. I feel that I am the main suspect; it turns out my parents had more money than I thought. I tried to explain that if the killing was Saturday night then we were together for the Nixon Library gig. Their answer was that he might have been shot very late Saturday night or even early Sunday morning. Then they added that I have no alibi for Sunday morning."

"Can't they track your cell phone or car computer chip to show that you were at home when your father was killed?" Leon Coyne asked.

"Maybe you ordered a pay per view movie at one in the morning?" Lee added.

"I'm going to give it a few more days before I go into panic mode," said Forrest. "Let's change gears, Saturday we are back in Yorba Linda. Their Sunrise Rotary is holding the annual lobsterfest function. This is a super gig unless you don't like lobster. I made sure that our contract gives us a table, and we get the same unlimited lobsters as the guests. Remember this function from last year?" added Forrest. "

"Ya, this group gets pretty lit up if I remember right.," said Leatha.

After going over the logistics for the gig, including the timeline, Forrest then said. "I want to show you a short video. I think it will be time well spent."

"Forrest it is too early for a porn flick," joked Shawn.

"Never too early and never too late." said Forrest as he pushed the play button.

Wearing a black t-shirt, the sixty-two year-old superstar fired out the opening beat of "We Take Care of Our Own": "I've been knockin' on the door that holds the throne / I've been lookin' for the map that leads me home" fired out Bruce Springsteen with more energy than a nuclear bomb. At the end of the song Springsteen and his E-Street band had energized Purple Cinnamon.

Leon shouted out, "That was the opening number of the Grammy Award night, you know when Whitney Houston died."

"Good job Lee." Forrest continued, "I wanted to give you a great example of rule one in music performances. You have thirty seconds to win over your audience. You have thirty seconds to engage them. Springsteen hooks the audience in five seconds.

"OK, let's go up stairs and try and get in a good two hours of practice," said Forrest as he lead the group from the den to the up-stars music room.

As Lee and Shawn grabbed their axes, Leatha went over to the Roland RD700NX. The Roland was a stage quality digital piano that was top of the line and gave a very professional onstage performance. Because it weighed almost sixty pounds, Leatha left it with Forrest.

"Before the downbeat, I would like to add one more thing. Leatha would you volunteer to be Purple Cinnamon's captain of categories?" asked Forrest.

"My husband Matt was in the Army, he told me that it is never a good idea to volunteer." replied Leatha.

"Since P.C. is not the Army, I think Matt would not mind. Leatha I would like you to help us by setting up categories for our music. I was thinking of four, but if you want to come up with your own groups, that would be cool. The categories I had in mind were 1. Performance ready, 2. Near ready, 3. Work in progress, 4. New song ideas. That way we can make sure that our time together is balanced. Guys, does that sound okay? Leatha, I will send you a email of the four categories and you can mess with it."

For the next two hours Purple Cinnamon reviewed the list of the three sets of twelve songs that they would need for Saturday night, and worked on the newer additions to their list.

As was their tradition they finished the jam with the B-52's "Love Shack."

If you see a faded sign at the side of the road that says

15 miles to the love shack' love shack' yeah, yeah......

Chapter 19
Crime Lab

DETECTIVE CLOUD ENTERED HER password into her office computer. She was anxious to see what progress the lab had made with respect to the evidence that had been collected at the Dupree crime scene. The Sheriff's Department had good case management software. The homicide unit also had a criminal analyst that was assigned to the unit to help coordinate the flow of forensic input from the crime lab and other sources. All this info would be fed into Detective Cloud's case management file. The software would take any DNA data and automatically run it through CODIS. That stood for the Combined DNA Index System. The system was funded by the F.B.I. and stored all DNA profiles collected from federal, state and local agencies.

Orange County public safety professionals were fortunate to have one of the nation's top forensic science laboratories in their backyard. The Orange County Crime Lab, or OCCL, was an ultra-modern one-hundred-thousand square-foot facility that had a staff of over one hundred and fifty. The lab had international accreditation in all major forensic science disciplines and was now a division of the Orange County Sheriff's Department. The lab had been a political football in the county and for several years had been co-managed by the Sheriff's Department, The DA's office and the County's C.E.O. A recent grand jury study recommended that the OCCL be turned over to the Sheriff's Department and made one of the department's divisions.

When the lab was called out on a case, the evidence was collected, inventoried and routed to the appropriate bureaus and units in the OCCL that specialized in that piece of evidence. Most evidence would first go to latent fingerprints and then, if it was gun related, it would be routed to firearms and tool marks.

The first thing that Christy looked for, after she logged in, was the inventory of collected evidence. The lab's list included latent fingerprints, a button, three cartridge cases, blood samples, one piece of toilet paper, two bullets, victim's clothes, and an envelope.

Results were posted on three of the items in question: vic's clothing, the three cartridge casings, and the two bullets that were dug out of the floor at the crime scene.

The lab report said that the collar of his polo shirt had traces of chemicals that were consistent with a gun shot from a distance of three or four feet. The pattern was constricted indicating the use of a suppressor. Blood samples from his shirt matched the blood of the victim. The victim's clothing did not disclose any hair, blood, or epidermis cells that were not those of Fred Dupree.

Christie then read the report on the three casings. This is weird, she thought as she tried to put the findings in perspective. A nine-millimeter fired from a Beretta 92FS, a .45 Caliber A.C.P. fired from a Kimber 1911 type, and a 357 magnum from a Ruger GP100 revolver. This is bullshit, she thought, how could there be a revolver casing at the crime scene? A semiautomatic pistol would eject each shell casing with each shot, but a revolver holds all five or six cartridges in the gun cylinder. You have to manually pop open the wheel and eject them all.

Detective Cloud had full confidence in the firearm unit of the lab. She knew they used the National Integrated Ballistic Information Network, or the NIBIN's, digital database to compare the microscopic marks produced on a cartridge case. The NIBIN was supported and managed by the Bureau of Alcohol, Tobacco, Firearms and Explosives. Christie read further, hoping that the report on the two found bullets that were imbedded in the floor would clear up the mystery.

The report continued. Two bullets recovered: both were 200 grain, Speer Gold Dot .45 G.A.P. HP. The lands and rifling marks indicate they were fired from the same Glock pistol. The condition of each bullet did not make it possible to be specific as to whether the firing gun was a Glock 37, 38, or 39. The report also indicated that the .45 casing found could not have held either of the bullets found.

With her head spinning, she reviewed what she had learned yesterday at the Dupree autopsy. If he had been killed with two large caliber bullets to the head, then what role did the 9mm cartridge casing play? Before she went face to face with Sargent Simcic she needed to get a better understanding of the ballistics report from the lab.

"Devon, This is Detective Cloud. I'm lead on the Dupree case and I just read your part of the report."

"Figured someone would call. Looks like we got a clever perp out there." he replied. "Why could the Kimber casing not be part of case?" Christie asked.

"Oh, it is part of the case, because it was found at the scene, but it did not hold the bullets recovered. Let me explain. In 2003 Glock wanted a forty-five that could have a small grip and still be a forty-five. Glock worked with Speer ammo and came up with the G.A.P. ammo. It is a small case, about the length of a 9mm but fat enough to hold a .45 caliber. It is just a Glock creation. It has not been a super seller, and the three Glock models are the 37,38 and 39. I always thought that Glock was hoping to get the departments to buy them for the female officers; The Glock 37 has a grip that is great for smaller hands. Detective, I'll give you my opinion. The vic was shot by a Glock 37, and the rest of the evidence is fluff. I mean I think the perp is just playing with our minds. I understand that the latent guys found something on the envelope and are about to run it through AFIS. Check your screen in next hour or so." continued Devon.

After thanking him she arranged a meeting with her partner Sandy Anderson and Sargent Simcic, but not before she reviewed the difference between an A.C.P. and G.A.P. cartridge casing on Wikipedia. She knew that the slob Simcic did not know the difference between a .45 caliber and the end of his dick, yet she wanted to be on her A game just in case.

Chapter 20
Tinson Rap Sheet

RETURNING FROM A COFFEE run, Christie ran into Investigator Anderson. She had been partnered with Sandy for the last year. They got along super, and Christie liked to share Simcic stories with her. Sandy had worked the jails for four years before she moved from custody to sex. Sex is cop talk for the Special Victims Detail. They still joke about her transfer to homicide and the first time she was introduced to Sargent Mike Simcic. The fat man spent almost an hour telling her he was a star at Servite High School, and could have been a NFL great except for his knee. He also told her he would have been Chief of Police in Eugene if they did not need him here in Orange County. If Christy had not calmed her down, she says, she was ready to return building C-17s with Boeing after meeting Simcic.

"Christie look at your screen before we go to the conference room."

"The lab got a good hit on the envelope.," said Sandy.

Oh shit, thought Christie as she read the latest from the lab.

The OCCL was able to lift a partial palm and a full finger from a number 10 envelope that had been retrieved on the side of the front porch. The National Automated Fingerprint Identification System or A.F.I.S. had matched the prints to a known felon.

Paco nmi Tinson

His Record of Arrests and Prosecutions

Convictions and failure to appear summary

Felony (s) 1: assault class C felony 5 years ago

Gross misdemeanors (s) 2: criminal trespass 6 years ago, DUI 7 years ago

Misdemeanor (s) 2: possession, possession with intent to distribute 10 years ago

also arrest 2 years ago, dismissed lack of evidence

Christie printed the report along with the Tinson's arrest and prosecution report and headed to the conference room for her case review with Simcic and Anderson.

Sandy was seated at the table but there was no Sargent Simcic. "I spoke to the Lab, and Devon who works firearms thinks that some of the evidence was planted by the perp," commented Christie. She started to repeat what the lab had told her when the Sargent came in.

"Cloud, you are lead on this case, what more do we need to charge that drummer kid with his father's murder?" barked Mike Simcic. "Let's get the kid in here and sweat him before he gets lawyered up. I want to be there; I'm busy this afternoon so let's bring him in tomorrow morning. Any problem working a Saturday, Cloud?"

"Sarge, can we go over the results we have from autopsy and the lab?" asked Christie.

Simcic said okay, but he first had to get a fresh cup of coffee before he would sit down and listen to Detective Cloud. For the next twenty minutes Christie and Sandy went over the up-dates to their case file. Mike was terrible listener, but to his credit he kept his mouth shut for most of the review.

"Christie, I don't get this .45 caliber issue. Why can't the .45 case found match one of the .45 bullets found?" She went over with the Sergeant the history of the Glock 37 and Speer ammo. "Ok I get it, and I agree with the concept that we have a lot of bullshit evidence," added Simcic.

"Sarge, the envelope with Tinson's prints are our the first solid lead. We need to pay a visit to Tinson and see what he was doing last weekend." said Christie.

"Cloud, Anderson, let me explain. That drummer kid has probable cause. He was playing his fucking drums in Orange County Saturday evening and he has no alibi late that night or early Sunday morning. Today he is about six million dollars richer!"

"The only connection to the Tinson guy is a piece of evidence that we all think was planted.," continued the Sergeant. "You two go to Lynnwood and see what you can learn about Tinson," said the Sergeant.

Just as the three were about to break up the meeting, Mike's Blackberry beeped. He looked down at the message and took a deep breath. "Shit, we got a double homicide in Laguna Woods. First Villa Park, one murder in twenty years, and now Laguna Woods, lowest crime in our cities. Now get this, possible husband and wife—seniors again. You two wrap up the Dupree case; get the kid in here in the morning. I am going to L.W.

"One more thing—the bastard also killed their dog." Simcic shouted as he huffed out of the conference room.

Chapter 21
O.C. Sherriff Invitation

FORREST'S CELL PHONE STARTED to do a little dance on the kitchen table and then the "Riders on the Storm" ring tone jarred him from his thoughts.

"Hey buddy, I just locked up your father's house, over all it is in good shape," said Shawn.

"Thank you," replied Forrest. "What did you find?"

"It looks like the only damage is with the entryway tile. A couple of tiles are chewed up from bullet holes and an area about three by three feet is stained pretty bad. Forrest, I took it upon myself to get some hydrogen peroxide and that seemed to remove most of the stains. I found a small area rug in the den and put that over the messed up tiles in the entryway. You will want to get a tile company to replace the entryway. The only other thing is dark dust from the crime scene guys who were dusting for fingerprints. That is about it, I don't think you will find any other surprises," explained Shawn.

Shawn continued to tell Forrest that if he wanted him to join him next week, to just let him know. Forrest figured that he would go to Villa Park next Tuesday. He walked over to brew a Keurig coffee, but his mind was thinking about going through his dad's house. It was going to be necessary to meet with an attorney in a week or two, so he could learn what he was supposed to do with his dad's estate. Before seeing the attorney, he needed to deal with the funeral home. It was just Tuesday that he had learned about his father's death, yet it felt like it was weeks ago. Forrest then wondered if he was supposed to cancel everything or if it was proper to try and go on with his life. Shit, he thought, what is the correct thing to do?

As he took his first sip of the Starbucks Pike Place Roast he heard his cell phone again.

"Forrest, this is Detective Cloud, O.C. Sheriff's Dept."

The first thing that Forrest thought was that they had caught his father's killer.

Christie continued, "We need you to come to the station tomorrow morning. Can we make nine a.m. work?"

"I guess so—but can I ask what this is about?" he replied.

"Mr. Dupree, we now have some of the lab results, and the quicker we get you crossed off the list of people who do not have an alibi, the more we can focus in other directions."

"What you are saying is that I am still a suspect in the death of my father," said Forrest.

"Look, lets meet tomorrow at nine so I can go over what we have from your father's autopsy and the stuff from the lab. Can we make that happen?" asked Christie.

"Should I bring an attorney?" Forrest asked. "Forrest, that is your call, but you are not under arrest."

"Ok, see you in the morning," he replied. Forrest continued to listen as Detective Cloud gave him directions to the station and parking instructions, but traffic would not be an issue on a Saturday.

Forrest pushed the speed dial for Shawn.

"Hi buddy, what's up?" answered Shawn.

"The cops want me to go to the police station tomorrow for questioning. Actually, it's the Sheriff Department on Flower Street in Santa Ana. My question is: Do you think I should get a attorney or what?" Forrest asked.

"Did they say why?"

"No, some bullshit about reviewing the evidence, and wanting to eliminate me as a suspect," Forrest replied.

"Look, I'm twenty minutes away from you and I am in my car—let me come over, we can pick up some take-out, and we can figure this stuff out."

"Are you sure that won't mess you up? Forrest replied.

Shawn told Forrest that he would stop and pick up some Taco Bell so long as Forrest would break out his hidden supply of Patron.

As Shawn finished his second chalupa he asked Forrest to tell him exactly what the cop chick had said.

After a couple of margaritas both Forrest and Shawn were in agreement that he should go one time to the sheriff's department. If it got serious, he should quickly shut up and lawyer up.

"Look," Shawn said, "we had a gig the night your dad was killed, you don't have a gun, and you had not been to your dad's house for weeks. Fuck 'em. Go to their department, give them thirty minutes and call an attorney if they pull any shit."

"Thanks Shawn, and thanks for coming over," Forrest said with deep sincerity. "Let's change gears for a bit. What did you think about having Leatha being captain of our music lists?" Forrest asked.

"Anything that will make P.C. more profitable or help us get some bigger gigs is cool. You and I are in agreement on treating our music business like a business." Shawn continued.

"We need to write our own music, that is the key."

"If we only cover the music of others, we never make the show," added Shawn.

For the rest of the night, the two lead members of Purple Cinnamon reviewed the few new songs that were works in progress, and made a commitment to launch a new song in the next couple of months.

Forrest and Shaun split the remaining fast food, and Shaun, with a bag under his arm, started for the door. "Forrest, don't forget, if the cops start to play hardball, just smile, shut up and lawyer up."

"Shaun, I have seen the elephant and heard the owl. This crap pisses me off, but does not intimidate me."

Chapter 22
Lynnwood, California

"CHRISTIE, YOU'RE NUTS. YOU can't be hot for a guy who is your suspect in your murder case." said Sandy, as she moved into the HOV lane on the westbound 91 freeway.

"You are just jealous that I said dibs first," responded Christie as she reviewed the Paco Tinson file. "The file doesn't say that Tinson is a ganger, but I think everyone who lives in Lynnwood do gangs." She wondered to herself the relevance of an envelope with his prints near the Dupree porch.

"What is our game plan with this guy? We could arrest his ass. We've got his latent print at a homicide and he is a convicted felon," Sandy tossed out.

"If we are going to bring him in we should get some uniforms to join us," Christie added.

"No, let's just push him a bit and then compare our observations of the guy. I don't think he will run—we can hook him up anytime."

Cops had their own vocabulary and special off-the-record code speech that they used between themselves. Some departments would substitute names to avoid criticism from the media who might have been monitoring their frequency. A large department in Georgia would substitute the name Canadians for African-Americans. If a patrol car saw a group of blacks hanging out on a corner known for trouble, they would radio to another car that a group of Canadians were gathering on 23rd and Monroe. Putting a pair of handcuffs on a perp under arrest was called hooking them up.

"Let's take 605 North, 105 West and we will take Long Beach Blvd exit," volunteered Christie.

"OK, then we can take M.L.K. Blvd, and will then get off on Bullis," added Sandy.

The Parks and Rec. Dept. seemed empty, but Christie and Sandy finally located someone that could locate Tinson. They left the building and walked over to the far side of the park where a skateboard mini-park was under repair. There were two guys there who could have been Paco Tinson.

"Paco Tinson?" asked Christie, looking at both of the park workers.

"I'm Paco. Who are you?" was Tinson's reply. Paco Tinson knew in a second that the two gals were cops. The Lynnwood park, were he was working, was a hangout for the Los Angeles County Sheriff's Deputies. He very well knew the ones who had the Lynnwood beat. These two were not anyone that he recognized.

Christie reached for her star and ID and held it up to him as she said, "I'm Detective Cloud and this is Detective Anderson, Orange County Sheriff. Can we ask you a few questions?"

Paco looked her right in the eye, but did not answer her question.

"You are Paco Tinson, correct?" asked Christie. Both Sandy and Christie were watching his eyes. "Ya, I'm Paco."

"You are employed by the City of Lynnwood, is that correct?" continued Christie.

The objective was to try and keep him in small talk for as long as possible and watch his eye movement as he answered basic, non-threatening questions. The goal was to keep the suspect from lawyering up and at the same time establish a baseline of the suspect's neuro-linguistic behaviors. The eye movements were the key. Most people would bring their eyes to the right when thinking of answers that were true. When they were asked a question to which they would need to invent an answer, they would need to go to the cognitive part of their brain and their eyes would move to neutral or, most of the time, to the left.

"When you go to work, do you drive or take public transportation?" continued Christie. As Tinson answered these simple questions, Sandy never took her eyes of him.

"Mr. Tinson, we had a situation in Orange County last weekend, specifically in Villa Park. Were you in Villa Park last Saturday or Sunday?"

Paco Tinson had never been intimidated by the cops, especially by females. Logic told him to just say nothing except I want to call my lawyer, yet he had been off the radar for several years, so he figured he'd let this go a little further.

"Last Saturday I was playing cards with a couple of friends," Paco answered as confidently as he could.

"When was the last time you were in Orange County?" Christie followed up.

Tinson looked her in the eye and said, "I have not been in Orange County for three or four months and that was the last question I will answer."

"Mr. Tinson, we want to thank you for your time." Christie said, as she and Sandy Anderson turned and left the skate park.

"He's lying, no question, lying," Sandy said as they headed to the car. "Text book, the soft questions he moved his eyes to the right on each question. When you asked about Villa Park and then Orange County, it was clear, his eyes went up and to the left. Absolute text book, he lied."

"I saw it the same way," confirmed Christie.

Chapter 23
Interrogation 101

FORREST LAUGHED TO HIMSELF as he was escorted to a standard police interrogation room, one with the old beat up steel desk, a couple of chairs and of course the window with the two way glass. He was no longer nervous; instead he decided to enjoy the bullshit. On the drive to Santa Ana he had worked through his own mental gymnastics. He knew he didn't kill his dad. There was no way in the world that the cops could frame him for his dad's death. Might as well relax and end up with a great story to tell for the rest of his life.

"Mr. Dupree, my name is Sergeant Mike Simcic. I understand you have met Detective Cloud. What can you share about your father's finances?" asked the Sergeant.

"I know that he and Mom did not have a mortgage on their home and that Dad had sold his business a couple of years ago," replied Forrest.

"With the death of your father, who will inherit his estate?" Simcic asked.

"I would assume I would unless he donated everything to the Girl Scouts," answered Forrest.

"Let me tell you something. We get dozens of murders every year where the motive was under five hundred dollars, hell last month we had a killing for fifty bucks and a bottle of oxy. It appears to me that a punk drummer would be highly motivated to kill his dad for five or six million."

Forrest did not provide an answer; actually he was not sure if the Sargent had even asked a question. He used the one or two seconds to mentally review his strategy. Forrest was determined to not let this fat cop push his buttons. He decided it might be the time to go on the offense. Just before Forrest spoke, he glanced over at Detective Cloud and was sure that he saw her roll her eyes.

"Sergeant, would you now take the time to review the results of my father's autopsy and results from the crime lab people."

"We don't release information on an ongoing case," Simcic replied sharply.

"Excuse me, Detective, did you not tell me that you wanted to review with me the status of this case?" asked Forrest, looking Christie in the eye.

"Yes I did," she replied. Simcic leaned back in his chair and brought his right hand up and rubbed his double or triple chin.

"Mr. Dupree, we do not have all of the reports from the lab, but we have some information that we can share. First, your father died from two gunshots to his head. He died instantly, and I feel I can say with confidence that he felt no pain. The lab is certain that both bullets were from the same gun. We are still waiting on several tests that take a little longer." Christie explained.

"Forrest, let me explain something to you. We are working your father's case very hard. We have to include you on the list of potential suspects. Family members commit a high percentage of homicides. That just is a fact. Second, so far you have the most to gain from your father's death. Now help us with something that will let Sergeant Simcic cross you off the list. Review with us everything you did Saturday and Sunday last week. Leave nothing out." said Christie.

Sargent Simcic pushed his chair noisily back from the table and got up and left the room. Forrest was sure that he was now stationed outside the two-way glass window. He resisted the temptation to flip him the bird.

For the next half hour he went through everything that he could remember about the last weekend. Christie took copious notes on a yellow pad. If TV crime stuff were correct then Forrest figured they were videotaping this meeting.

"Detective, I got home from our gig with the Boy's and Girl's Club about eleven forty-five or midnight. Why can't you do some sort of cell tower GPS thing with my cell phone?" asked Forrest.

"Hey drummer, this isn't a TV crime show." Simcic interrupted as he came back in to the interview room. "One more question," said the Sergeant. We show that you own a gun, where is that gun now?"

"What?" replied Forrest, "I have never owned a gun and I don't think my dad ever owned a gun, this is bullshit." replied Forrest in a loud voice.

"Kid, we're done today, but do not leave the state without calling this office, are we clear?" added Sargent Simcic.

Christie asked Forrest one more question. "Can you think of anyone who would want to harm your father? Take your time." Simcic left the room and Forrest sat back down and faced Christie.

"Detective, I have no knowledge of gambling, he drank a moderate amount of booze, and there no way he was into drugs. My dad has not been in business for years. He sold his business for several million, not sure of the exact amount, but that would not make anyone want to kill him. I am going to the house for the first time next week. Are you sure that this was not a robbery?"

"Forrest there was a Rolex watch next to his drink in the den. Also there was another watch, a Maurice Lacroix that was on a desk in his bedroom. That is seven or eight thousand in very fenceable jewelry. That is why we don't feel that the motive was robbery. If you know of something valuable that is missing let me know. Okay?"

As Christie walked Forrest to the main door on Flower Street, she added, "Forrest, you are a smart guy, think of something that would put you at your home on Saturday night. You know, a pay per-view, a fax, or something you ordered on Amazon."

He said he would work on it, and then walked to his car.

Christie walked back into headquarters and located Sargent Simcic. "Mike, Sandy and located Paco Tinson yesterday. He says he has an alibi for the time of the Dupree killing. Says he hasn't been to Orange County in several months. We both feel he is lying, and I think we need to focus on this Paco guy," explained Christie.

Christie was sure that she saw a bead of sweat appear on Simcic's fat forehead. He sat down on his chair and threw one leg over the corner of his desk. It took the Sergeant more time than normal to respond. "Why do you feel this Tinson guy is involved?" was his replied.

"Mike, it was a standard field interview, we developed a baseline with fluff questions and then when we asked about his activities during the time of the crime. His behavior gave clear signals that he was lying. It was a textbook reaction of someone who had a lot to hide. Sandy and I want to focus on this guy," explained Christie.

"I think you guys are off base on this one, stick with that drummer guy. I will look into this Tinson fellow and you keep the focus on Dupree's son."

"Sarge, I don't think Forrest had anything to do with his dad's killing," said Detective Cloud.

"What would be the motive for Tinson to kill old man Dupree? No reason, makes no sense, but the kid, ya, makes him the six million dollar man." Sergeant Simcic said with authority.

"Mike what about the envelope with Tinson's print? He's a felon and we have his print at a homicide," argued Christie.

"Christie, let me give you a course on Homicide 101," said Simcic in an arrogant tone. "You know why I am in charge of homicide? Because I know shit, and motive overrules any latent print. Cloud, I said and I would check out Tinson, you and Sandy focus on Dupree's son. Now get out of here—I need to get with the guys working that double down in Laguna Woods."

Once she was out of earshot of Simcic, she dialed her partner Sandy. "Sandy, you wouldn't believe how the pig acted during our meeting with Dupree's son."

For the next ten minutes, Christie told Sandy how Simcic made a disaster of the interrogation of Forrest. They discussed the hundreds of hours they have spent studying the nine steps of the Reid Technique of interrogation, the endless hours of role-play from confrontation all the way to confession. It was a system, but what was so frustrating to Christie was that Simcic acted like a freshman detective.

"Sandy, the pig was an amateur, and what made it worse was he did not want us to follow up on Tinson. This is a weird case. He said we are to focus on Dupree's son, and told me to back off on Tinson, that he would work him. I'll let you have your Saturday back, we can re-group Monday morning. If anything breaks I will give you a shout," finished Christie.

As Christie headed to her car, she noticed that Sergeant Mike Simcic's car was still in the lot. Good she thought, the fat man reminded her of skunk vomit. This case stinks...

Chapter 24
Lobster-Fest

THE ONLY THING THAT was upgraded on Forrest's wheels was the premium sound system. He had a cool Mustang for daily driving, but his 2007 Ford Econoline cargo van was his main drive when he had a gig. The E-250 was old school but the 4.6L V8 got the job done. The ample room in the cargo space was perfect for the drum kit that he used for gigs. Loaded in the back were twelve Ludwig Atlas Pro Touring bags filled with his various drums, cymbals, hardware and sticks. The Ludwig bags were black and red, but more importantly the drum bags had about one inch of foam to protect the precious cargo.

Most drummers are collectors; they love the latest and newest in equipment. Forrest drooled when he looked at the pictures in Modern Drummer, the monthly magazine for professional drummers. A picture of Rush's Neil Peart, surrounded by a zillion drums and cymbals, is a fantasyland for every man or women who picks up the sticks. The dilemma for Forrest was the time involved in setting up and taking down his kit, plus the hassle of loading and unloading the equipment from the van. His travel kit was made up of high quality Ludwig drums and Paiste cymbals. Forrest kept his gig kit conservative, an 18 X 22 Ludwig Legacy Virgin Bass, two floor toms, a 14 X 14 and a 16 X 16. Add to that 8 X 10 and 8 X 12 toms and a 6.5 X 14 Ludwig Legacy snare. In addition to his 14" Paiste hi-hat he brought three other Paiste cymbals and included was his favorite, an 18" Boomer China. The drummer even had a Ludwig bag for his Vic Firth sticks.

Forrest saw the exit sign for the Lakeview exit that would take him from the east bound 91 freeway to the city of Yorba Linda. He liked to be at a gig an hour and a half before the first downbeat, that gave him time to unload and set up and still have a half hour to visit with the key people who were putting on the function. Once he pulled into the Community Center he could feel his endorphins kicking in. The bullshit with the cops was now a distant memory. Forrest really enjoyed this part of his life, and it was not just the actual performance, but he enjoyed setting up his kit and just spending time with his band members.

Even though it was September, it was still eighty degrees out in the Community Center parking lot. The Rotary volunteers had been there for hours, and boiled lobster aroma filled the air. The night before, several members of the Yorba Linda Sunrise Rotary had gone to LAX and picked up seven thousand pounds of lobsters that had been flown in from Boston. They had the stage set up about thirty feet from the pots that were cooking the lobsters.

It appeared to the members of Purple Cinnamon that the crowd would be over twelve hundred. It was a coincidence that just last week that P.C. had played in Yorba Linda. This function was the biggest fundraiser of the year for the non-profit and Forrest understood that they could net forty or fifty thousand. One of the volunteers, a guy by the name of Nathan, said that all of the profits would go right back into the community.

Shaun and Leon had carried the Roland up to the stage and Forrest was seated behind his drums. It was time to rock and roll. Forrest was thinking about his band philosophy, you have got thirty seconds to wake up the crowd and get them to pay attention. The first song would be a wake up number.

Forrest liked to come out strong with the first couple of songs. Leatha would take the lead with a female version of "You Really Got Me," by the Kinks in 1964. "You Really Got Me" had fast changing power cords that would fire up most audiences. A male vocalist usually did the song, but in 1981 Helen Schneider had put out a great version. Leatha carried this song real well and Shaun, with his typical Boston Baseball Jersey, shorts and ball cap, let his presence be known as the lead guitar as he laid down the song's famous strong chords.

The Drummer

…You really got me

You really got me

you really got me…

It doesn't get any better than this, thought Forrest, as he gave the hi-hat a steady workout during the first verse and pre-chorus.

Eddie Cochran and his manager Jerry Capehart wrote "Summertime Blues" in the late 50's, but the Who's version kicked it up a notch. Leon and Shaun would do the vocals, giving Leatha a chance to catch her breath. Leon loved doing the low voice segment, especially the signature line: "I'd love to help you son, but you're too young to vote." This song was a great follow up to "You Really Got Me."

Purple Cinnamon finished their first set and took a break, while the Rotary event chairperson took one of the four mics and handled event logistics. Forrest used the time to get his charts ready for the second set, and then went over to the margarita stand and ordered a virgin margarita. On the way back to the stage he ran into Nathan, who told him that they had set eight lobsters aside for their next break, or after the gig if they wanted.

The rest of the evening went super, and there were still eight or nine couples dancing when Purple Cinnamon went into the final three mode.

Leatha had her sexy voice in ultra cool, as she knocked out the words to "Every Breath You Take."

Shaun and Leon were next with an amped up version of "Love Shack."

Forrest looked around and saw that nobody from Sunrise Rotary was coming up on stage, so he took it upon himself to close the evening.

"Ladies and Gentlemen, on behalf of the Yorba Linda Sunrise Rotary, we want to thank you for coming out tonight and supporting the Rotary and the Yorba Linda Community, Thank you again and please drive safely."

Shaun, turned off his mic and then said, "Forrest you are so on your game. Let's pack up, eat some lobster, and then go over to that bowling alley bar so I can buy you a real margarita."

Chapter 25
Candy Man

"Two is my maximum," explained Forrest, as Mitch Boseman bought the band another round.

"Leatha said you gave her a promotion, she is now captain of music."

"Mitch, your wife is captain of lists."

"I keep the master list of the songs we know and the ones we suck at," Leatha explained to Mitch. Her husband had joined up with them as Purple Cinnamon was wrapping up their final set.

Leon leaned into their table and said, "I am going to cruise the parking lot to make sure the bad guys are not eyeing our equipment."

As Leon went out the back door, Forrest leaned back and checked out the venue. Saturday must be karaoke night, Forrest thought. The bar had an Elvis theme, even though it was located in the middle of a community bowling alley. Forrest took a sip of his margarita, as a singer was doing a great rendition of "Candy Man." Forrest got Shaun's attention and said, "Check out 'Candy Man,' this guy is really good and he has down the best visuals or hand motions I have ever seen."

"He is good, and the D.J. does a superb Elvis. Forrest, he did Suspicious Minds when you were in the can, and it was better than Elvis did."

"There is some great talent here and I think most are locals."

Purple Cinnamon stuck around until the bartender made the last call for alcohol announcement.

Steve Thigpin was asleep in front of his T.V. in his Placentia home. He had broken the rule about having the best home in the neighborhood; his four thousand square foot rambler was located on the Alta Vista golf course. Even with a thirty percent hit in the real-estate market he figured it was still valued over a million. He choose to stay in the house after his messy divorce six years earlier because, he was not about to play the Alta Vista course and see his ex-wife screwing in his old house.

Morgan, Sawyer and Thigpin, LLC had been one of the most profitable law firms in Southern California. It was still a very successful firm, now operating under the name of Morgan, Sawyer and Lin. Morgan, Sawyer made a fortune for its partners litigating medical malpractice cases. Steven L Thigpin was the firm's leading rainmaker and chief litigator for many decades. Thigpin's share over the years amounted to tens of millions of dollars. It was no surprise that, twenty years ago, a hot thirty six year old blond with a load of silicon would target a distinguished sixty-one-year-old multi-millionaire attorney. After his divorce, Steve Thigpin put his energy into his golf game and occasionally mentoring the new kids at the old firm.

A small noise in the kitchen brought him out of his sleep. He was still dressed in his club's golf shirt, from the day's decent eighteen holes. He looked at his watch and figured it was too early to go to sleep and too late to go out to dinner. Reaching for the remote, he did not see a shadow emerge near his family room.

He was really pissed. Yesterday the cops from Orange County grind on him, and this morning he gets a call on one of his three burn phones. The call came through at seven in the morning, emergency, sixty thousand for a fast hit in Placentia. "No way," explained Paco, "I'm on the fucking radar."

"This is the last one for a long time, just get it done, that is why I added a extra twenty K. Look kid, with all this extra money you can quit dealing in those fucking pills. Do this one job and I will send your mom another twenty," shouted the caller.

For the next fifteen minutes Tinson took down all the details of the target. An eighty-one-year-old man who lived by himself on a golf course. After the call he broke the cell phone into small pieces and walked around his block, dropping the phone parts as he walked.

That night he would use a Ruger GP 100 .357 Magnum. A revolver that would chamber six cartridges; ether .357 magnum or .38 special. He had positioned the first two chambers to hold Federal .38 Super +P 115 gr. and the other four to hold .357 Magnum 158 gr. Hydra-Shok JHP. As usual he had adapted the revolver to allow a silencer to be attached.

Thigpin turned his head just in time to see the intruder take aim at his head. A double action revolver did not shoot as fast as a semi-auto, yet Paco's double tap took less than two seconds and both found their home in the head of Steven L Thigpin.

It was dark, but Paco could still tell that several rooms had fantastic views of the golf course. What a great way to spend retirement, he thought. You could sit out on your porch with a bottle of Don Julio 1942 anejos Tequila and watch the golfers all day long. I wonder if this house will sell at a discount because there was a murder here, he thought. Because the hit was so easy, he allowed the dust to enter his brain as he fantasized about buying the house. Normally he fought the dust in his brain, but tonight he could not get past the idea of trying to buy the house. Paco reached into his pocket and threw an empty pack of Salem 100 lights on the floor; he then left by the back door. He took the time to use the key he found on the inside of the door to re-lock the dead bolt to the back door. People were so stupid to leave a key on the inside of their dead bolts. He walked a mile down the golf course and hid near Kraemer Blvd, until a FTC brother picked him up.

Within an hour Paco was back at his apartment playing poker with three other gang members. "Let's see, we have all been here since seven tonight. At ten I ordered a couple of pizzas and we played until now," said Paco. "Looks like my luck was bad tonight," said Paco, as he handed out a thousand dollars to each person present.

After the last brother left, Paco used his regular cell to call DirecTV and order a pay-per-view.

Chapter 26
Retired insurance agent Kately, C.L.U.

"It happened again," he yelled as he jumped up and brought the O.C. Register over to his wife. "Two of my old clients killed within a week," Sid said as he charged into his little office where he kept files from his old clientele.

Sidney Kately, C.L.U. retired eight years earlier after a very successful career in the life insurance business. He was a lifetime member of the prestigious Million Dollar Round Table and also was a C.L.U. Less than five percent of insurance agent achieved both M.D.R.T. and C.L.U. credentials. The Million Dollar Round Table was awarded to those agents who were able to sell very large amounts of financial service products to their clients. The C.L.U. designation stood for Charter Life Underwriter, and it took five years of concentrated study to receive that designation.

Sid pulled the files of Fred Dupree and Dr. Harvey Flag, and returned with them to the kitchen table. He explained to his wife that both were long time clients and that he had read of Dupree's death last week, and now Harvey Flagg.

Sid had stayed with Victory Mutual Insurance Company his whole career. He brokered very few policies outside of Victory Mutual and the Dupree and Flagg cases were no exception.

After opening Fred's file, he recalled the case, a very large whole life policy sold to Fred's company. The file showed that Dupree

Environmental Solutions was the owner and beneficiary. The face amount was four million dollars, but after Fred sold his company, the policy was transferred to Fred as part of the transaction. Six months later Fred sold his policy to a viatical, or life settlement company, called Ruhall Settlement Group, LLC.

"My client Fred Dupree had a four million dollar policy that I sold, but he sold it to a company about two years ago," Sid told his wife as he closed the Dupree file and opened the Flag file.

Even before he opened the file, Sid recalled most of the aspects of Dr. Flag's case. He had sold a five million dollar policy to Dr. Flag many years ago. It was a great estate planning case; the doctor had bought the policy so there would be money to pay the I.R.S. for the estate taxes that would be due when he died. Flipping through the file he saw the change of ownership dated about two and a half years ago. Dr. Flag had transferred the ownership of his five million dollar policy over to Ruhall Settlement Group.

Sid set the file down and took a deep breath. "Karen, I have a weird felling about these two murders. This does not smell right. I am going to do something, but I am not sure where to start."

"Do you think you should call the police, or maybe Victory's home office?" his wife asked.

Sid Kately, C.L.U. made a decision. He remembered that Fred Dupree had a son who was still in the area and he would call him.

Chapter 27
Success Formula

FORREST WAS UPSTAIRS SEATED at his kit, not playing a particular song, but instead he was practicing. Somewhere he had heard that successful people are successful because they had formed the habit of doing the things that the failure did not want to do. For a drummer, it was practice. Years ago he had formed the habit of practicing at least five times a week. Forrest knew that only twenty percent of drummers would practice five days a week. In a success book, it said that if you do the same thing every day for twenty-six days, it would be harder to not do it than do it on the twenty-seventh day. That meant a habit had been formed.

The drummer set up his metronome and would work on the most basic of drum rudiments. The basic four are the single stroke roll, the double stroke roll, the flam stroke and the paradiddle. Sometimes Forrest would work on these rudiments on a fifty-dollar drum pad in the kitchen or den, but today he was seated at his kit working on a flam stroke. If there was a common success thread that connected all great drummers, it was their ability to keep time. It is one thing to stay on 104 beats per minute when you are fresh, but the thread of success is to maintain a perfect 104 bpm when you are tired. The key to the flam stroke is get one stroke to sound like an echo of the other. He held both sticks the same height above his snare, then lowered his left hand three inches and brought both sticks down at the same time: bam bam.

His concentration was so focused that he almost missed the vibration of his cell phone. Putting down his sticks he glanced at the name of the incoming call. As he answered the call, he could not recall the name Kately.

Forrest did not have a clue, that in the next five minutes, his life would change forever.

"Forrest, my name is Sidney Kately, I was a friend of your father's. Forrest, I hope I did not call at a bad time. You are not in the middle of lunch are you?" He told Mr. Kately that the time was fine and he had time for the call.

After giving his sympathies for the death of his father, he went on to explain the purpose of his call. Retired agent Kately said, "Forrest, I may be way out of line, but I felt I needed to call you with some information. Your father was a client of mine and I had sold him a large policy many years ago. I also sold a large policy to a Dr. Harvey Flag. Both your father and Dr. Flag were both killed within ten days. My records show that your father sold his policy to a company that buys policies from insured's who feel that they do not need the insurance any more. What that means is that with your dad's death, someone is collecting four million dollars. What is so alarming is that Dr. Flag had also sold his policy several years ago, and as a result of his murder, someone is going to collect five million dollars. Forrest, my records show that it is the same company that may be beneficiary of your dad's policy and Dr. Flag's policy."

"Mr. Kately..."

"Please call me Sid," Kately interrupted.

Forrest continued, "Let me see if I have this correct. My dad had a policy for four million dollars; he sold the policy to a company who will now collect on my father's death."

"Yes," answered Sid, "The policy was issued by my old company Victory Mutual. It was a whole life policy so it had a large cash value. Your father would have received more than the cash value from the company that bought it. The company that bought your dad's policy is Ruhall Settlement Group LLC. After buying the policy they would have continued paying the premium to Victory Mutual. At the time of your dad's death they would file a death claim and receive the four million."

Kately and Forrest continued discussing how the viatical or life settlement business worked. It was agreed that tomorrow, Forrest would look through his father's papers and see what he could find. Sid said that he would refresh his knowledge of the life settlement business and also try and get information on The Ruhall Settlement Group. It was agreed that they would talk on Wednesday after Forrest had looked at his dad's papers.

There was no way that Forrest could continue his practice session; instead he picked up the phone and called Shaun.

Chapter 28
Father's house

SLEEP HAD NOT COME easy for Forrest that night. Between the anxiety of going to his dad's house and all of the questions that had resulted from the call from retired agent Kately, he doubted that he had had three hours of sleep.

He parked his car in front of the house, took a deep breath and headed for the front door. Forrest had always had a key to his parent's home, but he could not remember the last time he had used it. Shaun had offered to join him this morning, but Forrest felt that he had to do this thing alone. If he was going to break down and cry, he wanted to be alone, and not in front of his best buddy. He turned the key, twisted the knob, and the door opened. Forrest looked ahead of the travertine entryway and walked right into the kitchen. He knew that he had walked on the rug that Shaun had placed on the blood stained and broken tiles, but he would deal with that later.

Forrest felt that he could play all the macho mental games necessary, but damn this was going to be hard. He was having second thoughts about doing this alone. Maybe if he could get some TV going or music, it would not be so difficult. He located a tuner and amp in the den and tuned to 88.1, the jazz station from Long Beach. Forrest had to laugh when he tuned in to KJAZZ and he got "When The Saints Go Marching In" by Louis Armstrong. The music helped, and he then decided to try and make some coffee. He remembered that he had bought his dad a Keurig coffee machine after his mom died, and he wondered if it was working. Working and well stocked, Forrest was armed with a cup of black and bitter, and he then headed to his dad's file cabinet that was located in the den.

Forrest found a bunch of files in the several areas: estate planning, life insurance and sale of D.E.S. Returning to the kitchen with his coffee and five pounds of files, he settled down to look for any documents that would reference Ruhall Settlement Group. He hit a home run in a set of papers in the life insurance file, a separate file named Victory Mutual and Ruhall. Forrest put that file on top and decided to bring the entire files home for review.

Forrest stuck around for another hour. The Rolex watch was right where Detective Cloud had said it was. Forrest located the other watch and then hid them both in a bedroom drawer. He realized that he needed to get all this stuff organized. This was now his home or at least his property; he had to get proactive with all this inheritance stuff. What he needed to do was get some help and devote two days a week on all the necessary paper work. This would be so much easier if he did not have to deal with those sheriff cops and their insistence that he was the prime suspect.

Back home, Forrest ordered a pizza and decided to plunge into this insurance business. As he went through the files and papers it hit him that he was going to have to deal with the IRS and all kinds of stuff. He realized two things, or maybe three things. He was rich, he needed to hire some help, and third, he was still a suspect.

Several hours later, he had separated all the papers and files into four stacks. The Ruhall transaction, tax stuff, miscellaneous things to do, and stuff that probably was not important, but that he would save for a year or two.

Forrest gathered up the big stack of Ruhall papers and took the pile to the den, where he studied them carefully for several hours. Several times he grabbed his iPad and looked up insurance policy terms on Google and Wikipedia. He felt he was ready for his call to insurance agent Kately tomorrow. Should he hit the drums or grab a beer and stare at the TV? The beer and TV won.

Chapter 29
Insurable Interest

SID KATELY CONSIDERED IT a well-earned luxury to sleep in until seven or seven thirty. For more years than he could count, he would be up by five thirty and be at the office by seven. After retirement he looked at a late morning wake-up as a reward. Today was different—it was like the old days—he was on a mission and he was at his desk doing more research by seven.

One of the basic principles or pillars of life insurance was the concept of insurable interest. During his whole career, he honored that concept. A stranger could not take out a life insurance policy on a stranger's life. An insurance company would not issue a policy if you tried to insure your neighbor and put yourself down as the beneficiary. When a person took out a policy on their life, they would have to name a spouse or child as the beneficiary. The only exceptions were business cases, and then the beneficiary should be their business or business partner.

The more he read about this life settlement business, the more it turned his stomach. He still received several professional journals and last night he looked-up all the articles he could find on this concept of selling your policy to a third party. In the old days, when you did not want or need your whole life policy, you just surrendered it to the company that issued it for its guaranteed cash value.

After two more hours of plowing through his files, journals and court cases on the Internet, he was ready to call Fred Dupree's son.

It was about ten in the morning when Forrest and Sid connected. Forrest told Sid that he had found lots of good info in his dad's file.

"Sid, you sold my dad his policy when he was forty-nine, and the annual premium was $68,245. The cash value when my dad sold the policy was $2,132,000. He was seventy years old. Sid that would have been a year after my mother died. We are talking two years ago. That Ruhall Company offered my dad $2,451,000. That's about $300,000 more than the cash value. There are lots of copies of forms for my dad to release medical information to the Ruhall Company. I found a copy of a check for $2,451,000 payable to my father."

"Good job, Forrest, It seems that your fathers situation is very similar to that of Dr. Flag's, except his was a five million dollar policy. I have a change of ownership form that was done at Victory Mutual home office. They sent me a copy because I was the agent of record. That took place about thirty months ago," explained Sid Kately.

"How do these Ruhall guys make money? They paid my dad $300,000 more than the surrender value of the policy."

"Forrest, they will receive the face amount or death benefit. In your dad's case, they will receive four million. That is a profit of almost one million six hundred, minus the two years of premiums to keep the policy in force."

"So they cleared a net profit of one million four hundred fifty thousand dollars." added Forrest.

"Here is what I learned about Ruhall Settlement Group, LLC. They are incorporated in the state of Washington. Their office is in Issaquah, Washington and the owner is Harold Ruhall. It looks like they have been a corporation for four years. I have address and some corporate papers that I found that I will mail to you," continued Sid. "Here is some additional information that I have found, and my theory about what happened to your father."

Sid shared with Forrest what he had learned. "The key for a settlement company to making money is the underwriting of the case. My research says that you need to be very accurate with your life expectancy evaluation. When the company makes an offer to buy a policy, they need to be right on as to when the person will die. Example: a seventy-year-old male has a lifespan projection of another thirteen years. That is an average; some will die in one year and some could even live for thirty years, but the average will live another thirteen years. If the life settlement company feels you are in bad health they will pay more for your policy and be more excited about the deal because they think they are going to collect on your death earlier. "What has happened is that these companies have not been very good at calculating when their new insureds will die. Two things have happened, and I feel this is what happened at Ruhalls."

Sid continued, "First, medical breakthroughs continue to keep people alive longer, and also the pre-baby boomers are really getting into exercise and good health habits. The second thing is this: these life companies use brokers to find and make the sale. These brokers have figured out a way to exaggerate the medical problems of their prospects. That way they make the sale and get their commission. The Life settlement company makes an offer thinking that the future customer is in worse health then they really are. They feel the person will die many years before they actually do die. The salesman lies to make the sale, but he does not own the settlement company, so he doesn't care.

"Forrest, I think this Ruhall Settlement Group has bought a lot of policies and continues to make premium payments to the insurance companies that issued the policies and nobody is dying. This is between you and I—I don't need a lawsuit at my age, but I would bet my last dime that Ruhall killed your father and Dr. Flag. That would bring in a fast nine million dollars and I think it is tax-free."

"Sid, I have a question," asked Forrest. "What are the chances this connection between my Father and Dr. Flag is just a coincidence?"

"Forrest, I was in the life insurance business for thirty years, and I was good. I had over fifteen hundred clients, and yet I have only had a dozen death claims. Most of those claims were deaths from illness or an auto accident. I've never had a murder. Out of all of my clients, only two sold their policies to Ruhall Company, and within two or three years they are both murdered. Forrest, would you get in line to sell your policy to the Ruhall Settlement Group?"

"Detective Cloud, This is Forrest Dupree. I know why my father was killed. I understand that a Dr. Flag was also shot, and I know why he was killed. Are you interested?"

"Forrest, what do you know of the Flag killing? It just happened. Look, when can we meet?" she asked.

Forrest explained that Purple Cinnamon was having a practice tonight at his home, and they would be done about seven thirty. Christie said that she and Detective Anderson would be there at seven thirty.

Chapter 30
Band practice

SHAUN HAD ARRIVED A half-hour before the scheduled five o'clock band practice. For the next few minutes, Forrest brought Shaun up to date about what he had learned about the life settlement business from Sid Kately.

"Forrest, you are not the only one who has gone to insurance 101 class. After you called me, I contacted the guy that sold me my life insurance policy. I had a two hour coffee meeting with my insurance agent this morning at the Starbucks in Yorba Linda. Actually, about three blocks away from our Saturday night gig. He said that this business of selling policies is now a cottage business. He told me, Forrest, that these companies are running out of people who want to sell their policies and that they are now paying old rich people to buy a big policy and then they will buy it off of them. I think he told me that some of this stuff went to the Supreme Court." Shaun explained. "The bottom line is I.R.R., internal rate of return. If a life settlement company buys a policy, they need the insured to die fast after they buy it, or it screws up their rate of return of their investment. He said that if a person sells their policy to a third party, they then have lots of people hoping they die real soon. Not a good thing," Shaun explained.

Forrest told Shaun that the cops would be there after their practice and it would be cool if he could stick around so he could post bail if he got arrested.

"Shaun, one more thing, Detective Cloud is my first dibs. When this bullshit is over I am going to hit on her." Forrest added laughing.

"Buddy, I think we have turned the corner. I am going upstairs and get my music face on," said Shaun as he took a beer out of the kitchen refrigerator and went up to the music room.

Leatha interrupted the practice with a suggestion. "Guys, as captain of music lists I have a report to make."

"Speech, speech, speech." shouted Leon.

"Fuck you, Mr. Coyne, I'm a Captain and you are not," shouted Leatha. "Gentleman, we have a song on our list of still working on, it is the Ventures' 'Walk Don't Run.' Let's try and have it ready for game time in two weeks."

Shaun spoke next. "Leon this is so cool for you and your bass axe, plus Leatha is correct. 'Walk Don't Run,' gives everyone a three-minute voice break. I like the idea of having one instrumental each set."

Forrest had left the front door unlocked and had put a note on the door telling OCSD to walk in and join the group up stairs. At about seven fifteen, Detectives Cloud and Anderson joined Purple Cinnamon. They found a couple of chairs and settled in to watch the final few minutes of their practice.

"Ok lets wrap this session tonight. 'Love Shack' here we come..."

As Shaun and Leon packed up their gear, Christie came up to Forrest and said, "Mr. Dupree, you guys are great. This has been fun, I wish Sandy and I had come a little bit earlier."

With a relaxed smile on his face, Forest replied, "Mr. Dupree was my father, would you call me Forrest?"

There appeared to be a long eye-to-eye connection between Christie and Forrest. Sandy started to laugh and said, "Guys, I understand we have some business to do tonight?"

After Leatha and Leon took off, Forrest, Shaun, Christie and Sandy sat around the kitchen table. Christie broke the ice, "You guys have any Patron? Just kidding, we are kind of on duty, but a coffee would be great."

Forrest had pulled a few of the papers from his dad's files. "Detective, I feel that my father and your Dr. Flag were both killed because of a life insurance scheme. My dad had a four million dollar policy and Dr. Flag had a five million dollar policy. The beneficiary of both policies is a small company owned by a Harold Ruhall who lives in Issaquah,

Washington. Ruhall or his company received or will receive nine million dollars from the murder of Dr. Flag and my father."

Sandy looked at Christie and said, "Interesting. Could you explain while I get myself some coffee?"

For the next hour, Forrest, with a little help from Shaun, walked through all of information they had.

"Let me see if I have this down," Christie said. "Your father had a big life insurance policy on his life and after your mother died, he decided he did not need it any more. Instead of turning it in to Victory Mutual and getting its value, he sells it to these Ruhall people who pay him much more then he would have received from Victory. These Ruhall Settlement guys make themselves the beneficiary and keep paying the premium. How am I doing?" asked Christie.

"Ya, all this paper work shows that is what happened. The speculation is that Ruhall Group got tired of waiting for my dad to die, so they speeded it up. Same for Dr. Flag." explained Forrest.

Shaun then added what he had learned the night before on the Internet. "This whole business of selling policies started years ago when victims of AIDS sold their policies to get money for treatment. The concept has grown from that. It can be a real money maker if you can buy a policy, make yourself the beneficiary and then have the insured die soon."

"Forrest would you mind if Detective Anderson and I stepped outside for a few minutes?" asked Christie.

"That will give me time to hit the head," replied Forrest.

"Sandy, what do you think?"

"In college I took a course that covered life insurance. I have a little understanding of what cash value is. Christie, remember cop rule 55, there are no coincidences. We have two shootings and they are connected." Christie thought for a minute and said, "Sandy, is it too early to ask Forrest for a date?"

After they both stopped laughing and regained their composure, Christie said, "Lets meet with the insurance guy tomorrow, and also I got a real funny feeling about how Simcic is pushing Forrest and is downplaying the Tinson guy. Lets keep pig face out of the loop for a few days."

Returning to the kitchen, Christie said, "Forrest, you and Shaun have given us some real good info. Can we keep the lid on this, and let Detective Anderson and I work through what we have so far?"

It was agreed that Detective Cloud would call Forrest in a day or two, and if he found any more pertinent information he was to call her direct.

During the drive back to Orange County, their conversation was split between the case, how cute Forrest was, and what a jerk Simcic was.

As they pulled up to Sandy's car, Sandy looked over to Christie and said, "Did you notice that lead guitar Shaun does not have a wedding ring?"

Chapter 31
White Rabbit

For the first time in over a week, Forrest felt that he was coming out of the fog. He felt that he could finally return to something close to a normal routine. Staying in shape had always been a priority for Forrest. A drummer needed to have strong arms and shoulders, and also to have legs that were strong enough to work the bass, or kick, and also the hi-hat for the duration of a performance. This morning he was going to use his dumbbells to give his forearms and shoulders a good workout. Out of habit he first went to his coffee machine for coffee and the bottom half of a bagel. He would have the remaining bagel half after his workout.

A small CD player was loaded with Miles Davis's *Sketches of Spain*. He liked this album because the track "Concierto de Aranjuez" played for over sixteen minutes. Working through his third set of twelve reps he was reminded of the story that Grace Slick used to listen to this same track and that it then inspired her to write the classic rock song *White Rabbit*.

As Forrest settled down in front of his computer, he wondered what time Detective Christie would contact Sid Kately. His goal that morning was to learn as much as possible about Ruhall Settlement Group and the guy that appeared to own it. Forrest started his search by bringing up the Washington State Secretary of State website, and was able to confirm that the LLC was incorporated five years ago. Harold L. Ruhall was listed as registered agent, with an Issaquah address. The WA filing date and expiration date indicated that the LLC was still active and also gave the assigned UBI number. All of this Forrest wrote down.

Forrest was about to start his search for Harold L. Ruhall when his phone rang. "Hey Forrest, it's me Leatha. I did not know if you knew, but another senior was killed. A lawyer by the name of Steven Thigpin was shot in the city of Placentia." After getting as much information as Leatha had, Forrest figured he should call Sid and find out if the attorney was also a client of his.

He went ahead and called Kately who informed him that he was talking to the sheriff detectives right then.

"Let me keep this quick. An attorney by the name of Thigpin was just shot in Placentia. Sid, was he one of your clients?" Sid said no, and Forest told him to share the info with Detectives Cloud and Anderson and to also to tell them hello.

A Google search resulted in a lot of good hits. It seemed that Mr. Ruhall had gone up through the ranks with the Northeastern Surety Life Insurance Company. First hired as an agent who made the Million Dollar Round Table in his first three years. He was promoted to a management position and was an agency manager in their Portland Office. Harold then became the Regional Vice President of Northeastern Surety's Western Regional. The final four years of Harold's NESL's career was in the position of Senior Vice President of Marketing.

While Forrest took a break and refreshed his coffee, he had a thought. Instead of continuing his search of Ruhall, he decided to try and find any survivors of Steven Thigpin. An Internet phone book yielded three names in the area with a Thigpin in the name.

The first call was a dead end and resulted in a lecture that the guy he called was on the national do not call list. Next he placed a call to Riverside, California and was connected to Steven Thigpin's daughter. Initially she was skeptical, but warmed up when Forrest explained that his father lived in Villa Park and was also shot last week. Forrest explained to Sonia Thigpin Martin that he need to find out if her father had any life insurance. Mrs. Martin said she could call her father's friend who is still with the law firm and has been helping her dad with legal stuff. Forrest gave her his phone number and e-mail and told her to get back to him any time of day if she found anything out.

For the rest of the day, Forrest split his time between digging into the life of Harold (Hal) Ruhall and trying to organized his father's estate material. It was clear that his father had a lot of money and also it was also clear that it was going to take weeks, maybe months, to figure it all out.

The other thing he was able to learn was that Ruhall had a wife and that her name was Maureen. Maureen Ruhall lived in Issaquah, Washington, in a nice house about five minutes from the office of Ruhall Settlement Group.

Chapter 32
Nine million dollar motive

SID KATELY AND HIS wife Margaret lived in a modest ranch style home in Anaheim Hills, about two blocks off Kellogg Drive, near Esperanza High School. Christie and Sandy had made arrangements to meet about nine thirty in the morning. Margaret had brewed a fresh pot of coffee and had blueberry muffins set out.

"Good morning officers, my name is Sid Kately and this is my wife Margaret. Please come in."

Sid walked the two detectives through his information. He was very clear to break his information up into two parts, the first was material that was factual, he had proof to back up what he presented. This included the documents that proved that Fred Dupree had sold his policy to Ruhall Settlement Group. The second part was his opinion or theory as to what happened. Lawyers or law enforcement did not intimidate Sid, not with his thirty years of business. He presented his theory professionally, yet he was very opinionated about what happened to his clients. "Officers, I am one hundred percent sure that Dr. Flag and Fred Dupree were killed so someone could collect nine million dollars."

Christie and Sandy were just about to thank Mr. and Mrs. Kately for their time when Sid said there was one more thing.

"It has now been almost two weeks since Fred was killed. I would recommend that someone calls the claim department at Victory Mutual and have them flag the claim and make sure they do not mail out a four million dollar check to these Ruhall people. I have the number for you if you would like it." added Sid.

Detectives Cloud and Anderson drove east on the 91 freeway. Christie asked Sandy, "Tell me what you are thinking?"

Sandy hesitated and then said, "I am sold on Kately's thoughts. It sure solves the problem of motive. Nine million is pretty good motive, even in Simcic's book."

"Simcic is another issue, but let's meet with the guys who are working the Flag case," said Christie

Morgan and Urqheart had been a team in the homicide unit for six months. Bobby Morgan had been working homicide cases for three years. His long time partner had retired six months ago and Frank Urqheart had come over from custody.

"Bobby, what do you make out of this stuff from the crime lab?" Frank Urqheart had read over the report and was puzzled. McDonald's garbage was left, and yet no 9mm cartridges.

"Frank, the part I find weird is all the residue of methyl ethyl ketone and toluene," answered Bobby. "Let's find Cloud and Anderson—they are anxious to compare notes with us." "Sargent Simcic feels that the son of the Dupree case needs to be considered as a possible suspect for our Flag case," commented Urqheart.

Christie let Morgan take the lead as he went over the evidence that had been collected at their scene. He explained that both Flags had been shot twice in the head in two separate rooms and a dog had two bullets in the chest. During the meeting, Morgan received a message that the toluene and ketones appeared to be from carburetor spray. For forty-five minutes the four detectives reviewed their cases looking for any similarities. Cloud and Anderson had not yet revealed the insurance angle.

Christie made the point that all the victims had been shot twice in the head. She also brought up the point that the shooter picks up all his brass, and then pretends to leave evidence. "He's fucking with us, Dupree was shot with a .45 GAP and he leaves a .45ACP, 357 from a revolver, and a 9mm," mentioned Christie.

"Our guy fires six 9mm, picks up all the brass and then dicks with us by leaving McDonald's cups and a pile of soup cans," was Morgan's input.

"Looks like they are connected," said Urqheart.

"Here is why we think you are correct," voiced Christie. Twenty minutes later Morgan and Urqheart were briefed on the life insurance documentation.

"We need to tell Sargent Simcic right away," Frank Urqheart said with urgency. "That is your call, but Sandy and I want to see if there is a connection with the Placentia killing and do some more work on Paco Tinson."

"Gee, the sergeant said Tinson should not be on our radar, that we should work with you guys and focus on a Forrest Dupree."

Twenty minutes later, Bobbie Morgan had agreed with Christie and Sandy to move Tinson to the front of the class. They also agreed to use the department's resources and follow up on Ruhall Settlement Group, LLC.

Detectives Cloud and Anderson hung around the conference room and discussed strategies that would crack Paco Tinson's role in the case.

"What we can agree on, is that the perp does a good job of keeping a clean crime scene and then deliberately leaves bullshit evidence," Christie told Sandy.

"The big question is: was the envelope that was found outside by the door left there on purpose like the rest of the stuff, or was it a mistake?" asked Sandy.

"My bet is Tinson screwed up," answered Christie.

"Morgan and Urqheart said that Tinson had a solid alibi for the time of Flag's shooting. He was playing cards with four other guys all night." was Sandy's input.

"Let's do this. We have enough with the print to get a judge to give us a warrant to check on Tinson's cell phone activity," explained Christie. Sandy said she would work up the paper work and have the D.A. find a friendly judge.

While Christie and Sandy were staying behind in the conference room, Frank Urqheart made a beeline to Sargent Simcic.

"Boss, Cloud and Anderson found this retired insurance agent who has tied our Flag case with their Dupree case. They think a company in Seattle killed them both to collect insurance. I am not sure I understand it all, but they are sure the Villa Park and Laguna Woods are connected," rambled Frank Urqheart.

"Damn it, this sounds like bullshit, Urqheart. Tell Bobbie to get his ass in here."

Chapter 33
The Lotus Girl

DRIVING OUT OF ISSAQUAH and getting on the 90 west gave Hal Ruhall a shot of adrenaline. Before he transitioned to the 405 north, he would stop at the Factoria Keg Steakhouse and Bar for a drink. The Lotus Girl Gentleman's Club would still be there after his cocktail stop at the Keg. Hal wondered about the history of local politics and the decision by cities to not grant liquor licenses to the strip clubs. Because the Lotus Girls did not serve liquor, he would just stop at a few bars as he made the forty to fifty minute drive.

Hal ordered a Bombay Sapphire martini and let his mind look back to the prior couple of weeks. The last ten or fifteen days had been the most stressful of his business life. He had retired from a great run with Northeaster Security Life. During the last four years of his Northeaster career he was bringing in about eight hundred thousand a year, and the best part of being the Senior V.P. of Marketing was a virtually unlimited expense account. After retiring, he was able to use four million of his own money as seed money for Ruhall Settlement Group. On paper, his business plan seemed perfect. He was involved in several company strategy forums that had researched the viatical and life settlement business. He knew the business, and this venture should have been a cakewalk.

He asked the bartender for another, this time straight up.

Hal took a glance at his gold Presidential Rolex and went back to his thoughts. Six months ago he had hired a consultant to review the business plan and portfolio of cases. After four days and six thousand he was given the bad news. Major insurance companies wanted to insure thousands of policyholders every year who they felt were in great health. If there were an underwriting error, it would be absorbed by the law of large numbers. It was explained that in Hal's business, he wanted to buy the policies of sick people. And because Ruhall Settlement Group was not buying thousands of policies they needed to be extra thorough when doing their underwriting. If too many healthy seniors were part of their portfolio of purchased policies, they would go bankrupt.

The consultant told Hal that his best broker, the one in Southern California, lied on the applications, and he also was able to get the insureds to go along and exaggerate their health condition. The bottom line was that it appeared that Ruhall did not have enough money to keep the policies in force until the insureds died.

The Keg Steakhouse and Bar was located at the intersection of the 90 and 405. Driving North on the 405, Hal pushed the button on his Sirius radio and tuned it to the Playboy channel. He half listened to the sex banter and let his filthy mind go back to that day in Bobby's backyard. The way Bobby's aunt pretended not to see him and continued to soap her large boobs still caused an instant erection. Maureen, his wife, had a very good body for a fifty eight year old. Her three or four times a week trip to the gym had minimized excess fat or flab. He had to be honest that she had a good rack and looked like she was in her mid forties. They only had sex about once maybe two times a month, and the only way he could keep it up was to think about Bobby's aunt or the big fucking tits of Gigi at the Lotus Club.

The Pandora Adult Cabaret was on the right as he drove north on Lake City Way. It was new and was probably a good strip club, but because it was smaller that the Lotus he doubted they had any larger women who had massive breasts. Five minutes later, Hal approached Bothell Way N.E., which was just a continuation of Lake City Way. He passed the famous Deja Vu Club and looked ahead to the sign for the Lotus Girls club.

Gigi had worked at the Lotus Girl for several years, starting after her career ended as a manager in local Washington Mutual bank. Who would have ever thought that WaMu would be brought down by the financial meltdown of 2008? She felt lucky, most of her friends and co-workers had lost their homes, and of course their economic security.

She worked three days a week, but if management called and said that Frankel was coming in, she would get a fast sitter and get to the club. On an average night she would make three hundred to five hundred. If Frankel came in, it could be a twelve- or fifteen-hundred-dollar night. On a normal night she would give the night manager twenty-five percent, because he was the guy who could steer her to a heavy roller or deep pockets. Girls who worked at a strip club were independent contractors, and actually had flexible hours.

Tonight, Hal went directly to the desk and was greeted by a manager he did not know. "My name is Frankel, and I called for a V.I.P. room with Gigi." As usual Hal did not use a credit card and instead handed over five hundred and he was then greeted by Gigi who escorted him up the deep plush merlot carpeted stairs, to the little private room. A special sign was above the door that let every patron know that it was the V.I.P. room. Of course, the V.I.P. room had a video camera, as did every square foot of the Lotus Girl. A high percentage of customers thought that a few extra hundred-dollar bills would let them cross the line at a club. That might work at a massage parlor where a happy ending was not uncommon, but strip clubs owned by large corporations were money machines, and they were very strict with their rules. If you pulled out your dick, security would calmly escort you out the door. That is why they always nailed your credit card before you entered a private room.

Gigi asked Frankel if he wanted a coffee or soda and he said a cola would be great. She was back in a few minutes with an ice bucket filled with three Diet Pepsi's and two glasses. His credit card was charged thirty-six dollars. Most clubs had one music system for the whole club, but the V.I.P. rooms at the Lotus had their own sound system. Gigi asked Frankel if he wanted U2 and Hal said yes. Gigi was still covered in a silk cover up as she went over to the music control pad and programmed U2's *No Line on the Horizon*.

"Frankel, I want you to lean back and close your eyes. I have just taken off my clothes; I am your friend Bobby's Aunt. I am now in the basement shower." Gigi had entertained Frankel for over six months and had heard his fantasy many times. "Okay, open your eyes." She had removed her cover up and was now naked except for a small G-string. Gigi was a very large women, her asset was she had extremely large tits, perfect areola and nipples that protruded about three quarter of an inch.

For the next fifteen minutes, she danced to U2 and pretended to rub her large breasts as if she was soaping them down in a shower. She would dance up to a few inches of Frankel's face while pretending to rub both the underside of her boobs and then twirl her fingers around her erect nipples as if she was soaping every inch of her beauty. Frankel knew the rules, he never raised his hands to touch her, but occasionally he would give his johnson a little rub. Gigi knew just when to dance in the direction of the CCTV so that the security team would not be alerted. After five songs she asked Frankel if he wanted to talk. She went over to the music pad and lowered the volume of the album a bit. Remaining topless she opened a Pepsi and poured herself half a glass.

"I was hoping that you would come in this week. How has everything been with you?" Gigi asked as she sat down next to Frankel.

Hal answered, "Worst week in twenty years."

"Tell me about it," replied Gigi.

Hal told her that sometimes people have to pay the price for not telling the truth. I had to make some tough decisions last week. He then continued. "Twenty six years ago I was on a business trip to L.A. I was in a bar and picked up a Hispanic girl at closing time. We went to her apartment and stayed in bed for the next twelve hours. I was so blitzed that I gave her my business card. She called me two months later and said she was pregnant." Hal took a drink from his cola and noticed that it was loaded with booze. It was not uncommon that the girls in a VIP room would sneak drugs or liquor to their customers, especially if they had deep pockets.

Hal kept talking. "For the last twenty-six years I have provided support. I have sent thousands to Juanita and our son Paco." He took another drink from the fortified coke and asked Gigi to do another dance. Gigi went to the pad and entered *Need You Now* by Lady Antebellum.

As Gigi did a private lap dance for Frankel, she told him that she was really turned on by how he had confided in her. While she danced she said, "You know the rules, you can't touch me, but would you object if I pleasured myself right here as I dance for you." For the next several songs Gigi lifted one large breast after another to her mouth. Her tongue circled her nipples while her free hand went down deep and sensuously rubbed her clitoris. Hal finished his drink and took a chance and slipped his hand down his pants and jerked his dick to a quiet explosion. Gigi had made sure that she was blocking the closed circuit TV system. Gigi almost fainted as her body was rocked by a massive orgasm. She had done thousands of private dances and hundreds of private rooms, but this is the first time she ever pleasured herself at the Lotus Girl.

Gigi sat back down and finished her soda. "Tell me about your son Paco." she boldly asked.

"He is a good kid, I have seen him twice. He helped me out big time this week, I owe him big." Hal got up and headed for the red curtain of the private room, " Hope to be back within the week." He reached back through the curtain and handed Gigi another three-hundred cash. "Thank you Frankel." she whispered as he left the room and walked out of the club.

Chapter 34
North to Seattle

The Purple Cinnamon had all agreed to come over to Forrest's house and try and get a handle on the status of the investigation of his father's murder. Shaun was the first to speak and told the group about the meeting between himself, Forrest and the sheriff detectives. He explained the theory of retired agent Kately and the mechanics behind a person selling their life insurance policy. Shaun had decent knowledge of insurance, and has really dug into the world of life settlements and viaticals. Leatha had explained that she had to leave by eleven as she had an open house in Brea. "I could have Matt cover me, but this is a listing that I fought for, for over a year," she explained to the guys.

"We will talk fast and then call you tonight and let you know of anything that you missed," added Forrest.

Before Leatha had to go, Forrest and Shaun brought everyone up to speed and Forrest provided all of the information he had learned about Hal Ruhall. Shaun then asked to present an idea. "Leatha, you need to get out of here. Real fast, here is my idea. Leon and I jump on a plane tomorrow and fly to Seattle. I already checked and there are lots of flights on Alaska Air. Also Leon's work is quiet now and my baseball stuff will let me get away for a few days."

Leon worked for School Fundraising Unlimited. His job was to work with school PTA's and come up with fundraising programs. Leon had been in overdrive from the middle of August to the middle of September launching all the new fundraising programs at his assigned schools. Now that his fundraising launches were over, he could break away.

Forrest then said, "Guys, I am humbled that you would do this for me, and I understand why I cannot go, but are you sure that you want to go Seattle?" For the next few minutes Leon and Shaun convinced Forrest why it made since for them to go check out the guy who might have killed Forrest's dad.

After listening to Leon and Shaun, Forrest said, "There is one condition. If you are going to check out Ruhall, then we are going to do it first class and professional. You have to agree to let me underwrite the cost. Guys, you know I will soon have my hands on a lot of money. Please let me cover all of the expenses. Is that a deal?"

Monday morning, Leon drove over to Shaun's house. Leon's girlfriend agreed to dog sit for Sparky, Leon's four-year-old Springer Spaniel. Right on schedule, a town car arrived and within thirty minutes they were walking up to the Alaska Air terminal and entering their codes into the kiosk at the counter. Shaun told the Alaska attendant that they had no luggage to check. Both Leon and Shaun pulled their computers out of their carry on and placed them in the plastic tub. As usual Shaun was wearing his ball cap, Boston baseball jersey and his signature Converse Hi-Top All-stars with black laces. There was a little line backup as Shaun undid his laces and put his shoes and ball cap in another plastic bin. Both Shaun and Leon were able to get through the machine without beeping. It appeared that the only people who beeped were seniors, many over seventy, who had artificial hips or knees. "Shaun, this TSA shit is really stupid, they are doing full pat downs to old ladies and men, and they are afraid to look twice at people from the middle east who are between twenty and thirty," whispered Leon.

While Shaun and Leon were doing the TSA dance, Forrest received a call from Sonia Martin, the daughter of deceased Steven Thigpin. She said that she had contacted her dad's attorney and he had referred her to the CPA who helped her father with his taxes and accounting issues. Sonia explained that the CPA had told her that her father was upset after the divorce and that he was able to sell his large life insurance policy to a firm that bought policies.

"Sonia, this is really important. I feel there might be a connection between both of our father's murders. I need you to do one more thing, this is important. Please call the CPA back and get the name of the company that bought your father's life policy. Can you do that?" Forrest pleaded.

"I will be back to you today," replied Sonia

Shaun and Leon had made reservations at the Silver Cloud Inn just outside of Issaquah on the I-90 freeway.

"Why are we using Budget?" asked Leon.

"Forrest had some rapid something card and it was easy to book on-line," replied Shaun. It was agreed that Leon would drive and Shaun would be navigator. Shaun entered the Silver Cloud address located on Southeast Eastgate Way in Bellevue into his GPS application.

"We will stay north on 405 until we jump on I-90, look, the Boeing 737 plant. I think all 737s are built there," Shaun explained.

"Have you seen this many fir trees in your life?" Leon noted. Not only did they have a great view of the Bellevue skyline, but beautiful fir trees lined both side of the freeway.

"Look at all the CCTV towers. I have never seen so many cameras in my life," Shaun interjected. "Leon we are at exit 9, we want exit 11. Look for Honda of Bellevue," Shaun added. "This is it, Factoria Mall. We are very close to the Silver Cloud Inn."

Leon and Shaun had checked into their room, grabbed a burger at the Burger King and were back on the east I-90. The scenic drive included fir trees with a mix of alders, maples and madronas and ahead of them was a fabulous view of the Cascades. Shaun said, "Leon, let's stay on this road. My phone says we are heading to North Bend and Snoqualmie Pass and we can be in Eastern Washington, and that means wine."

"After we meet the famous Ruhall," Leon responded.

"Shaun, exit 15, Lake Sammamish Park. Do you know what that park is famous for?' Leon asked.

"Go for it."

"In the mid seventies, Ted Bundy found two of his victims there, and months later the girls' bones were found where we are going, Issaquah." explained Leon. "Maybe this Ruhall guy will turn out be a serial killer," added Shaun.

After taking one of the exits for Issaquah they found themselves cruising down Front Street into the historic down town of Issaquah. Old style street lamps lined Front Street. Each one had a double arm that extended away from the lamps that held a large hanging plant.

"This place is really nice. What is a jerk like Ruhall doing in a cool city like this? Look—the Issaquah Brew House, twist my arm."

"Relax Shaun, after our work is done."

It only took a half an hour to get the lay of the land. Front Street, Sunset Way and Rainier Blvd. appeared to be the main drags.

"Shaun, take a picture of those cool looking salmon statues," shouted Leon. The Issaquah Salmon Hatchery was built in the thirties, and was located on the Issaquah Creek. Each year the hatchery raised over four million Coho and King Salmon. They were carefully released into the Issaquah Creek and wound their way to Puget Sound and then to the North Pacific. The graceful Coho salmon statues of Gilda and Finley were over eight feet long and made of bronze, making them a favorite for the Hatchery's thousands of visitors each year.

"Look for East Lake Sammamish Park Way southeast and southeast 64th Park Place." directed Shaun. A four-foot high concrete monument sign on each side of the street marked the entrance to the business park. The business park gave the appearance of being upscale. Leon pointed out that about a half of the offices were medical, and the other half were a mix of legal, accounting, and insurance.

"There it is." Shaun pointed out. Ruhall Settlement Group was on the second floor of one of about six free standing buildings. Each building had approximately six or eight tenants. There were not many cars parked in the parking area assigned to building three, the building that had Ruhall Group as a tenant.

"Forrest, Leon, How fast can you find a pay phone and call Seattle?"

"A pay phone? This is the twenty-first century. Wait, I think there is one at the AM-PM down the street."

"We are parked outside Ruhall's office. Want you to call his office and tell whoever answers the phone that you are calling from building two and it appears that Mr. Ruhall's car has a flat tire," said Leon, with a smile. Shaun poked Leon and said he wanted to talk to Forrest.

"Hey it's me, Leon wanted us to have a single king bed, but I got the room changed to two queens. Wanted you to know what out bassist is like out of town. Also we saw two eight foot salmon trying to hump each other in downtown Issaquah. Boss, we're going to get our masters degree on this Ruhall fucker. Anything new at your end?"

Forrest explained to Shaun and Leon that he was waiting for a call from Thigpin's daughter about what company bought his policy.

Forrest was able to find a pay phone, and used a phone card just purchased, to call the office of Harold Ruhall. After two rings, administrative assistant Stephanie Coke answered the phone.

"Ruhall Settlement Group. We are happy for your call—may I help you?"

Chapter 35
Ruhall Settlement Group

HAL LOOKED OVER THE paperwork that he was handed and allowed a smug smile to grow on his lips. His staff had filled out the death claim forms for Steven Thigpin. This claim would go to the Mutual of Pennsylvania Insurance Company. Mutual of Penn was a superior company, and he was sure that the claim would slip through without a problem. Six months ago, Hal had moved the ownership and beneficiary from Ruhall Settlement Group over to another shell company, this one called Zodiac Settlement Solutions.

Harold Ruhall had spent his whole business career in the insurance business. His ten years in the home office had given him the opportunity to understand all of the different departments. The good news about being assigned to the home office was that you got so serve on lots of different committees, the bad news of a home office assignment was that you served on lots of committees. Hal understood how a large company processed their death claims. A quality insurance company worked hard to pay claims. Contrary to media coverage, insurance companies took pride in their integrity with respect to claims. The big ones even kept records on how fast they paid a claim.

The one thing an insurance company did not want to do was to pay a claim twice. This could happen if they paid out a claim and then the courts required that they pay the claim to another beneficiary. Homicide death claims were flagged, and sent to claims specialists who gave those claims extra attention. If a claim was for an amount over a million, then it also went to a specialist. Hal felt the claims people who looked at Thigpin's claim, which had Zodiac as the beneficiary would not cross reference it with Flag or Dupree, because that was a Ruhall claim and it was with a different insurance company. Hal felt very comfortable that his bases were covered.

"Mr. Ruhall," said Mrs. Coke, "The people in the other building called and said you might have a flat tire, do you want me to call Triple A?"

"Shit, no, I will take a look."

"Look, there is our boy. Yes, as I expected the BMW is his. Cool, let's call Forrest and tell him we IDed Ruhall." Shaun said, as he reached for his cell. "Forrest, good job, we saw the bastard. Looks about sixty, polo shirt, and about five foot ten, under six feet. He walked around his car twice and walked back up to his office."

Leon and Shaun decided they were going to hit the Issaquah Brewhouse and try the local brew and also have a sandwich. After a couple of beers they would check out Ruhall's house.

Leon and Shaun were in their element at the Brewhouse. They had a couple of great microbrews and the Rogue Soseji Sampler. "Leon, let's try the Kobe Blue Balls," said Shaun as he finished his second beer.

They spend about an hour at the Brewhouse, taking in the local atmosphere and getting a little nourishment, if beer and Kobe Blue Balls are nourishing. Leon said in a quiet voice, "I could drink here all evening, but I kind of remember that we are on a mission."

"Yeah let's find where Mr. BMW lives, he might be home by now," said Shaun as he left the money for the meal and tip on the bar.

Chapter 36
Titty Bar

"We are looking for 194th Ave.," Shaun volunteered. Shaun had found Ruhall's address and was able to check out his house by doing a Google search. "Leon, take a look at this, 6,000 sq. ft., three stories and on the lake." The most expensive homes in the Issaquah area were on Lake Sammamish, and it appeared that Hal Ruhall did not want to go second-class. "Seems to me that his pad is ringing the bell at more than two million. Get as close as you can, and we can get up close by foot," continued Shaun.

"What is our bullshit, if the cops come?" asked Leon. "We live in Southern Cal, part of a rock band, and checking out real estate in the Northwest." responded Shaun.

After parking the car, they found the address and walked down the driveway. The driveway was about a hundred feet long before it circled the front of the three-story house. Alternating pine and Arctic pine trees bordered the narrow road. Ruhall's home was almost invisible from the main road. Shaun and Leon walked to the end, close enough to see the house, garage, and a glimpse of the lake. "Look, there is his BMW, the same one we saw at the office," whispered Leon. Standing in the shadow of a large lace leaf oriental maple, Shaun took in the setting and tried to figure out their next move.

Hal had finished his dinner, and headed to the family room to catch up on the news and go through the day's mail. His wife, Maureen, picked up the dinner dishes and tidied up the kitchen. In two years Hal and Maureen would be celebrating their thirtieth wedding anniversary. During the previous five years, Maureen had felt that she was just going through the motions. She had her civic activities and also served on the board of the local Issaquah YMCA. Hal had his business, and god knows what, she pondered. It was eight o'clock and she was debating whether to join her husband in the family room, or take a book down to the den. The book won. Maureen stuck her head into the family room and told Hal that she was going to try and finish the book that she was reading. Without turning in his chair, he told her that he was tired and might doze off.

After Maureen had left and headed out of earshot, Hal dialed the number to the Lotus Girl. "This is Frankel, Gigi is there tonight, correct?" asked Hal.

"Yes, Mr. Frankel, she will be here until one," was the receptionist's reply.

Shaun and Leon were about halfway up the driveway when they heard the BMW start. "Fuck, its Ruhall, there is no way we are going to get to the top of the driveway ahead of him." proclaimed Leon. They figured they had two maybe three seconds to get off the road.

"Here, between these trees, I don't think he will see us," whispered Shaun. A large Japanese black pine might provide coverage from the headlights of Ruhall's BMW. Both Shaun and Leon held their breath as Hal Ruhall slowly drove up his driveway. He passed within five feet of their hiding spot and continued to the main road.

"That was close. Come on, let's see where the jerk is going," Shaun said as he jumped up and started jogging back to the rental car.

"He turned right, I think we can catch him," encouraged Leon. Because traffic was light at this hour and Lake Sammamish Parkway had few turnoffs, they were able to spot and settle in behind the BMW. "Well, it doesn't look like Hal baby is going to the office, he has turned on the same freeway we took from the airport." Leon said. The BMW had distinctive taillights, which made it easy for them to follow Ruhall and still maintain a safe distance. "This is going to be a bummer, if he is going on a business trip and we end up at the airport," said Leon. "Maybe he has a suitcase of guns and is going to drive to California and speed up his death claims." "Look, he is turning off, we are in the area of our motel. He is pulling into a bar," commented Shaun. "Leon, go follow him and try and figure what he is up to."

"Yeah, I need to take a leak anyway."

"So do I, but I will wait for you, so he does not see us together," added Shaun.

"Dinner?" asked the receptionist. Leon told her he was going to just go to the bar and also asked the location of the restroom.

Ruhall was seated at the left end of the bar. He was dressed in jeans, a green polo shirt, and a high quality leather jacket. "Rum and Diet Coke," Leon told the male bartender. He chose a bar stool three down from Hal. It seemed to Leon that Hal was well known to the employees. Leon took a mouthful of his cocktail and headed to the restroom. With nobody in the john, he spit his mouthful of rum into the sink. Upon returning to the bar he was relieved to see that Ruhall was still there and working on his second martini.

"Ok buddy, it is your turn, he is in the bar, left side powering back martinis straight up. The can is in the hall that leads to the bar. The place is called the Keg, looks like a nice steakhouse. Also he has a green polo shirt and leather jacket." Shaun took a glance into the bar, saw Ruhall and went directly to a needed visit at the urinal.

Shaun nursed his Manny's Pale Ale. The bartender had told him that it was from the Georgetown Brewing Company, a Seattle microbrewery that put out a superb product. Just as he was getting into the bar menu, he saw Ruhall throw down some cash and head to the restroom. "Leon, wake up, I think he is on the move. We've got to come back here—they have a super prime rib burger. See you in a minute." Shaun left a third of his pale ale, dropped a ten on the bar and joined Leon, who had started the car.

"Forrest, are you watching Monday night football? Leon and I are moving to Seattle and opening up a private investigative agency," joked Shaun. For the next half hour, Shaun and Leon gave Forrest the rundown on the trip to Hal's house and their current trip north on Lake City Way.

"Hot damn," shouted Leon. "The SOB is going titty bar hopping. Forrest won't believe this."

"Let's drive past and then circle back so he doesn't spot us." directed Shaun. Leon parked the car a hundred, maybe a hundred and fifty feet from Hal's BMW. He then dialed Forrest.

"What's our budget? The bad guy has just gone in to a gentleman's club," explained Leon.

"A what?" replied Forrest.

"You know, a titty bar, strip club. It is called the Lotus Girl Gentleman's Club." was Leon's answer.

Shaun and Leon decided to stay in the car and wait Ruhall out. "Leon, look at the faint red glow on the corners of the building, they have this lot under the eye of big brother. I see at least three infrared CCTV cameras."

Chapter 37
Thigpin Policy

"Mr. Dupree, this is Sonia Martin calling. I hope I did not call you too late?"

"No problem, Monday night football, and it's only half-time. I appreciate you calling back, and please call me Forrest."

"The CPA got back to me and was able to get the information on my father's life insurance. He said that my dad was so pissed after the divorce, that he wanted to make sure that she didn't get the proceeds of his insurance, so he sold the policy. The company that purchased the policy was called Zodiac Settlement Solutions. The accountant said it was a LLC, whatever that means."

Forrest wrote that name down and then replied, "What have you learned from the police?"

"It seems that the Placentia Police Department are in charge. They have been real nice. I got a call from both the Chief and Deputy Chief and they gave me the cell phone number of the detective who is assigned to the case," replied Sonia.

"How are you and your family doing? It has to be tough," asked Forrest.

"I am feeling a little guilty. I got upset that my dad married a trophy wife. But I will say, that my dad was a super grandfather to my three kids. That is the hard part, explaining to them that grandpa has gone to heaven. I have a super husband, and he stayed close to my dad. That helps."

"Sonia, you have my condolences, and again I thank you for getting me the info on the insurance stuff. I am sure our sheriff people will be in contact with the Placentia P.D."

"Shaun, I hope you and Leon are spending your time writing Purple Cinnamon's next hit."

"Hi boss, we are still sitting outside the Lotus Girl. I checked my phone and there are a whole bunch of titty bars in this area. We may have to stay a week and do some in-depth research," joked Shaun.

"I am going to check in with the Sheriff detectives and see if they have anything new. Call me if Ruhall leaves the club."

Shaun replied, "What you are saying, Forrest, is that you are horny, and you are going to call Christie Cloud."

"Goodbye," said Forrest, laughing.

"Detective Cloud, this is suspect Dupree, I hope I have not called while you are on a hot date with Sargent Simcic?"

"Forrest, I was thinking of you. And no, I am home alone, with a glass of wine, and listening to the Jazz music station on DirecTV."

"I am doing Monday night football, but thought I'd check in with you."

"Cool, replied Christie, what have you been doing?"

"You know that Placentia shooting, the retired lawyer, Thigpin, Steven Thigpin?" asked Forrest.

"Yeah, that one is Placentia, but I saw it on the county activity log," replied Christie.

"I took it upon myself to call the daughter of the victim," explained Forrest. "It took a day of phone calls, but she, her name is Sonia Thigpin Martin, lives in Riverside, told me that her father also sold his insurance policy. She got me the name of the company that bought it. I was hoping it was Ruhall Settlement Group. It wasn't, some company called Zodiac Solutions or something."

"But Forrest, what are the odds of three shootings in two weeks and each victim had large policies and all sold them to third parties, instead of cashing them in?"

For the next fifteen minutes Forrest and Christie discussed his call to Sonia and what he had learned about Harold Ruhall. Then Forrest told her where Leon and Shaun were.

"Forrest, you guys are fucking crazy. Are you telling me that your friends are stalking Ruhall right now as we speak, outside a Seattle strip club? I don't believe it."

"Christie, are you mad?"

"No, but I am worried about you, Forrest. You're screwing around in the big leagues. This guy might be a serial killer. Call your friends, who is it, Leon and Shaun?" Forrest said yes. "Forrest, please tell me you will call them and get them on the first plane back to Orange County."

"Okay, okay. Stay on the line. I will give them a call."

"Christie, I called them. They said that Ruhall just walked out of the club. They are not going to follow him anymore. They said they would catch the next flight in the morning, but that they were going into the Lotus Girl to check it out."

"Forrest, promise me you will let me and Sandy be the cops and you will be the good drummer boy?"

Christie and Forrest spent the next half hour talking about how she became a cop and how he gave up a management career at J.C. Penney to form a band. "I want to see some of your pictures when you were throwing the javelin at USC," asked Forrest.

"Only if I get to see your high school pictures before you bleached your hair and grew your cool goatee. Forrest, you know you look just like that famous TV chef that has the cooking shows. The one by the name of Guy."

"Christie, while we have been talking, I was messing with the computer. You wouldn't believe what I found. I went to the Washington State Secretary of State website. You can enter a corporation's name. I entered the name Zodiac Settlement Solutions. I found it; it came up. Address is Issaquah, Washington, and Harold Ruhall's name is listed as the LLC member. Christie are you still there?"

"Yes, my mind is spinning. Forrest, you are amazing. Sandy and I need to be in Lynwood tomorrow. I will call you late morning. Forrest, one more thing—thank you for calling me tonight."

Chapter 38
Therapy

HAL KNEW HE WAS fooling himself, but he justified his trips to the Lotus Girl, like spending a grand with a psychiatrist. Tonight, he just was not in the mood to spend an evening with Maureen. There was so much about his business that he could not share with her, that it was just easier to not bring up Ruhall Settlement Group business at home. He wondered if their relationship would have been different if they had been able to have children. During the first five or six years of their marriage, they had gone to specialist after specialist and the consensus was that Maureen had something called polycystic ovary syndrome. This was one of the reasons that Hal felt that he could not tell Maureen about his son from a prior life.

"Mr. Frankel, nice to see you sir. Gigi is waiting for you in the VIP room. If you will allow me to run your card, or will tonight be cash, Mr. Frankel?" He did not say anything, but he had been in the Lotus Girl over twenty times and the majority of the time he did not use a card.

"Cash please," replied Hal.

Hal pushed the curtain aside and entered the small but cozy little room. Gigi had already ordered an ice bucket and was pouring a soda as he entered. After taking off his leather jacket, he made himself comfortable on the small sofa. "Frankel, can I pour you a coke? I can make it special." Hal knew that she was taking a big chance sneaking liquor into the club, but he figured that the higher tips more than compensated for the risk.

"Thank you. A coke sounds good," he replied.

Hal always told himself that this would be the last trip to the Lotus and Gigi, but his perversion was too strong. No matter how hard he tried, he could not escape the mental fantasy that had been with him for almost fifty years. Watching Bobby's Aunt through that basement window had triggered his young hormones and they continued to rage even forty years later.

Gigi asked Frankel if he wanted a dance or did he just want to relax and talk for a while. Hal said a little U2 music and a couple of dances would kick off the evening. Gigi had no intention of telling this client, but she had received a call from Washington Mutual, actually Chase, who had acquired WaMu's branches, and they had a position for her. She hoped that this would be the last week of the Lotus Girl and maybe even Frankel. Gigi removed her cover-up and was now only wearing a small bikini. She knew that her large frame and enormous breasts made her a sort of freak show at the club. Most of the girls were slender and at least half had silicon tits. Regardless of her size, she did not have any problem, getting her share of private dances at the club. Some clients like Frankel, had fetishes and requested only her. As "Angel of Harlem" finished, she took a sip of soda and got ready for "All I Want Is You."

"I remember what you told me about looking in the window and watching your friend's aunt taking a shower." Gigi said as she sat down next to Frankel. "If I had seen you watching me showering, I would have called you into the house. I would have asked you if you were spying on me and if you should be punished. I would have had you pull your pants down and put you over my lap for a spanking. Of course I would make sure I was only wearing a bathrobe when I spanked your bare bottom. Needless to say my bare breasts would be clearly visible to you during your spanking. Do you think you would have enjoyed that?" Gigi asked. Hal could barley answer as a giant erection was throbbing in his pants. The fantasy of being eighteen or nineteen and having Gigi give him a bare bottom spanking took his breath away. For a few seconds, he thought he might faint.

"How about one more dance?" asked Hal. "Certainly," replied Gigi as she entered a new song in the system.

"How have the last few days been?" asked Gigi as she poured Frankel another drink. She knew that the name Frankel was a phony name, just like her stage name Gigi. All of the girls had phony names. Storm, Temptation, Ebony, and Bambi were the favorites. "Busy, but I think business will be very good in the next few weeks."

"How have things been at home?" she asked, leaning a little closer to him and looking him right in the eye. Hal, or Frankel, took another drink from his spiked Coke.

"Things seem a little tense at home, it is like we are entering a cold war."

"How does that make you feel?" inquired Gigi.

"I told you I had a son in California. It was never appropriate to share that with my wife. The fact that I have this big secret is like a rock in my shoe. That issue, my secret family, acts as a block, I think, to normal relationships and communication."

"Tell me more," Gigi asked.

"I have thought about coming clean with her, but now that would be impossible."

"Why would it be impossible?" she asked.

"Things have gotten complicated between my son and I. I have had him do some work for me that is not exactly kosher."

"You said his name was Paco, how old is he?"

Hal had not realized that he had told her his son's name. It was good to be able to get some of this stuff off his chest, but it could also be dangerous. How ironic that he could not talk to his wife, Maureen, but he could share deep secrets with a topless dancer. If Maureen could just play along with his sexual fetishes and fantasies, maybe he would be at home tonight, instead of spending five hundred dollars in this creepy little room. "My son is in his twenties, how about that special shower dance that you do for me?"

After a couple of more dances, Gigi sat back down and opened another soda. "I got a call today from a bank, I might go back to bank management," Gigi volunteered. She wasn't going to say anything, but it just kind of came out.

"What would you do in banking?" Hal asked.

Gigi replied, "Branch management or loan officer."

"What do you know about finance or business?" Hal questioned.

That really pissed her off. She was not sure why, but she found his question so condescending. What did this asshole think, that she was born a fat topless stripper? She probably knew more about banking, leverage and loans then this pervert Frankel or whatever his name was.

Gigi figured she better get up and fake her way through another dance, or she might say something she would be sorry for.

Hal looked at his watch and figured it was time to head out. It would take him almost an hour to drive back to Issaquah. Even though Hal was a little high, he knew he had said something that had made her mad. He peeled off another hundred-dollar bill and thanked her for the sodas.

"Frankel, thank you, and drive safe tonight, okay?" Gigi said as Hal walked through the red and gold curtains of the VIP room.

Chapter 39
Gigi

"WE PROMISED FORREST THAT we would not follow Ruhall anymore, but that does not stop us from checking out the Lotus Girl," Shaun said as he got out of the car. The BMW had left the parking lot a few minutes earlier, and they figured he was probably heading home.

"Welcome to the Lotus Girl Gentleman's Club," the receptionist said to Shaun and Leon.

"Hi, our friend, the guy who just left, leather jacket, green shirt, said we need to ask for his special dancer," Shaun said.

"Oh, that's Frankel, he always asks for Gigi."

"Yeah, I think that's who Frankel recommended, yeah Gigi. Is she available for a few private dances?" asked Shaun. They were instructed to have a seat while the receptionist spoke to the manager on duty. A few minutes later Gigi appeared.

"I understand that Frankel gave you my name. I would assume that you would want the VIP room like Frankel. That is $300 for a half hour or $500 for an hour. Beverages are extra. If you are friends of Frankel's, I'd love to do a little dancing," explained Gigi in a quiet sexy voice.

Leon and Shaun agreed to a half hour and were escorted to the VIP room, after of course the club charged their card with the customary $300 charge.

"Guys, let me go over the Lotus Girl's rules. First we have CCTV cameras everywhere, so there is not an expectation of privacy. We cannot touch, and soda is priced at six dollars a can. The good news is the ice is free. The VIP room has its own music system with over three thousand songs."

"Gigi, my name is Shaun and this is my friend Leon. We have something important to ask, and I would hope that you would hear our story before you decide if you want to help us. We are not friends of Frankel's. His real name is Hal Ruhall. Gigi, Leon and I play in a band called Purple Cinnamon. Our drummer's father was killed two weeks ago, and we are trying to help him."

"My god, that is terrible, but I don't know how I can help," responded Gigi.

"Thank you," responded Shaun. "Gigi you are under no obligation to help us, but let me add. Four people and a nice dog have been killed. We think you can help us save some more lives," explained Shaun in a voice smothered with sincerity.

Leon then added, "we have reason to believe Ruhall, or as you know him, Frankel, has been involved in these crimes. Can you please share with us everything you know about Hal Ruhall? You might be able to save lives."

Gigi took a few minutes to collect her thoughts. As a businesswoman she was always good at keeping a problem in perspective. One of her assets was that she did not get overly emotional when analyzing an issue. Everyone has an initial reaction of not wanting to get involved. But that was one of the reasons the world was in such a mess. If more people trusted their instincts and held firm to their core values, we would not have gangs taking over our cities, and so many problems in our public schools.

"Gentlemen, I will help you if I can. I will answer your questions. Is it okay if I keep my clothes on?" she asked with a sheepish smile.

Leon smiled and said, "Ah shucks, this is my first time in a strip club."

Everyone laughed, the ice was broken, and for the next fifteen minutes Gigi told Leon and Shaun everything she could think of about Frankel. She even told them about his proclivity toward full-bodied women with very large breasts. Gigi felt that if she could save lives, she was going to give it one hundred percent.

"One more thing. During the last few weeks he has felt bad because he had to get his son Paco to do some dirty work for him."

"Gigi, we want to thank you for helping a lot of people. I think tonight we have saved some lives. This is our band business card. This is my cell phone number and let me write Leon's cell also."

"Guys, my name is not Gigi. My name is Carol Maddox. Here is my three-year-old WaMu business card, I still have a few left. My cell number is still the same. Keep the card, it will be a collector's item some day," Carol said laughing. Please don't use my real name around here. We girls like to keep our privacy, some of these clients are very creepy."

Shaun and Leon got up to leave, "Gigi, is it customary to leave a tip?" Leon asked.

"Not this time, and guys, I am glad you came by tonight."

"Leon, if the Keg is still open, I want one of those Prime Rib Burgers and some straight Patron."

Chapter 40
Century Station

THE PROTOCOL BETWEEN LOCAL police departments is covered in procedure manuals and years of cooperative tradition. Over the last several years, the level of cooperation had substantially increased, not just between local police departments, but also between the police departments of major universities and the local sheriff or police departments. The City of Lynnwood, while incorporated, contracted their public safety needs from the Los Angeles Sheriff's Department. Christie had called ahead and spoken to Captain Fallon Foss. Captain Foss had the leadership position at the Century Station on Alameda St. in Lynnwood. Not only did the Century Station cover public safety for the City of Lynnwood, but it also housed the Century Regional Correction Facility.

Christie explained to the Captain that they wanted to use one of his interrogation rooms to conduct a non-custodial interview. She shared with Captain Foss that they had a couple of murders in Orange County and that Paco Tinson was a person of interest, but they were not close enough for an arrest. Foss volunteered that his guys knew Tinson, because he worked for the City of Lynnwood in Parks and Rec. He also added that he would have an arrest team available to help them out, if their work uncovered any firm evidence.

Today it was Christie's turn to drive and she and Sandy hoped that they had timed the interview so they could avoid the westbound 91freeway crush.

"Christie, were you surprised that Tinson agreed to a non-custodial?" asked Sandy.

"Yes and no. This Paco guy seems smart, and they're the ones who like a challenge. They think they can outsmart a polygraph. I am sure he feels that he can outsmart a couple of female cops and then we will leave him alone."

When police have arrested a person or placed a person in custody, they are required to give the suspect their Miranda rights. In a non-custodial interrogation or interview the individual is not in custody and is free to leave anytime. Sandy and Christie were not planning to divulge to Tinson that they had his latent print from the scene. The print would allow them to secure a warrant or even place Tinson under arrest, but just a fingerprint found outside of Fred Dupree's door would not get a conviction.

"Sandy, our goal today is to focus on his alibis for the Dupree and Flag homicides. We are not going to let him know about the print. We might be sticking our foot in it, if we get into the Thigpin case, we will let the Placentia PD work that one up. Sandy, I am not sure what to do with this life insurance issue. If Paco killed Flag and Dupree, then the insurance people must have hired him. The question is how do we tie Tinson to the Ruhall people? Let's just work on his alibis and keep the latent print and the insurance close to the vest," explained Christie.

The Orange County detectives had signed in with the front desk and were killing time waiting for Tinson. The Century Station was one of the busiest and highest profile stations in Southern California. In 2006, the jail had been converted to an all female facility.

Paco Tinson entered the station like he was running for mayor or did not have a care in the world. As Christie and Sandy approached him, a L.A. Sheriff's deputy came over and escorted the three to one of the station's interrogation rooms.

"Mr. Tinson, we want to thank you for coming in today. We want to make it very clear that you are here voluntarily, you are not in custody and you can leave any time you want," Christie explained.

"I understand, how can I help?"

During the next five minutes, Sandy and Christie verified Tinson's address and date of birth and just shot the bull. It appeared to Christie that Paco was not as defensive as he was the other afternoon. They could not help but observe his tick or affliction that caused him to jerk his chin to his right shoulder. It seemed to be some nervous disorder. Maybe the guy had a form of Tourette syndrome.

"Again thanks for coming in. Paco, we have a homicide that took place in Villa Park about ten days ago. We have several suspects and you are one of those suspects. We have been able to scratch some others off of the list and we hope to remove you from that list as well. What were you doing Saturday the 9th between six p.m. and six a.m. Sunday morning?" Christie asked in a non-aggressive way.

"Playing cards with friends at my apartment," replied Paco.

"Thank you. How many in the poker party?" asked Sandy.

"Four plus me, a total of five."

"When did the game break up?" Christie followed up.

"I think one maybe one thirty. Can't you check my cell phone GPS thing? It will show that I was at home."

"Good idea, Paco. We would like to get you off the list. What is your cell number?" Sandy asked.

Both Christie and Sandy kept the conversation going as casual as possible. After getting Tinson's cell number, they secured the names and phone numbers of his poker buddies.

"This is very helpful, Thank you. Just a few more question and then we will be done. On the 13th there was a homicide in Laguna Woods. Can you provide an alibi for your whereabouts on the Thursday evening? We are talking about the 13th," asked Christie.

"Yes, I was home that night, maybe a little reading with ESPN on. I don't remember what game was on, but I like boxing and football," volunteered Tinson.

"Maybe we could verify that you were at home by doing a check of your cell phone, like you recommended," said Sandy.

"Yeah, I like that, especially if that gets me off your list. I have been clean for five years and I have a solid job with the city."

Detectives Cloud and Anderson thanked Tinson and they walked out together from the Century Station.

"Sandy, let's see if the Captain is in and thank him."

Both detectives returned to the station and located the Captain. They thanked him for the use of his facility and gave him an abbreviated update. "Captain, we are going to get a warrant and see if his cell activity matched up with his alibi."

Driving back to Orange County they kept imitating Tinson's tick.

"Sandy, I am going to call Forest and see if he is back from the airport with his band guys," she said as she kept jerking her chin to her right shoulder.

"Christie, stop that, you are going to get us in a wreck," yelled Sandy as she started laughing and also did the Paco tick jerk.

"Forrest, it's Christie and Sandy, where are you?" Christie asked.

"I picked them up about fifteen minutes ago, I will be home in thirty minutes. Christie you guys have got to come over, Shaun and Leon hit a home run." Forrest answered with excitement in his voice.

"See you in thirty or forty minutes at your house." agreed Christie.

"Sandy, hitting a home run is a positive thing, right?"

"Depends what team you're on." Sandy replied.

I wonder what team Simcic is on? thought Christie.

Chapter 41
Ask Forgiveness, Not Permission

"LT GENITO, DETECTIVE CLOUD here, my partner and I are returning from L.A., where we interviewed a suspect on the Fred Dupree case."

"Detective, bless, you. The City Council is eating me alive. You know how Villa Park is? They go bananas if we get a car theft. This murder has them thinking that they want to put out a RFP to Anaheim or raise taxes and get their own P.D."

Incorporated cities had one of three choices: contract with the Sheriff's Dept., maintain their own police department, or have a neighboring city cover their public safety. Yorba Linda had had the City of Brea cover their city for many years and then changed to the Sheriff Dept. Placentia had their own department, and of course Villa Park was covered by the Orange County Sheriff's Dept.

"Chief, I can imagine the pressure you are under. We think we are close to a big break on this case. I hope to call you tomorrow, so you can give your people some positive news."

"Detective, I hope you are right. Your Sergeant thinks you are barking up the wrong tree."

"Chief we will report back to you real soon," replied Christie.

"Sandy, pig face is going to be the death of me. I hate that fat fart."

Just as Christie and Sandy pulled up to Forrest's house, her cell phone rang.

"Cloud, Simcic. What is this bullshit about life insurance? You and Anderson get back to the station so we can coordinate with Morgan and Urgheart. They think the Dupree kid may have killed the Flags to throw us off. Where are you, and how fast can you arrive at the station?"

"We are leaving Lynnwood and will be there in a hour and fifteen, Sergeant."

Christie and Sandy joined Forrest, Shaun and Leon in the den.

"Are you guys nuts?" Sandy said before she had even sat down.

"Sorry, but we kind of have the philosophy of ask forgiveness, not permission." responded Leon.

"The problem as I see it, is that Ruhall or at least his companies, are tied to a minimum of four killings. A person who has committed four killings does not have a problem adding two more murders if they feel threatened," Christie said while looking at both Shaun and Leon.

Realizing that Sandy and Christie had to get to Orange County, Shaun and Leon told their story about going to Hal's business, home and the Lotus Girl.

"Here is the deal. Ruhall has spent a ton of time with Gigi, real name Carol Maddox. She was very clear that he has had some business problems in the last few weeks. She says that Ruhall told her that he feels bad about having his secret son, do some dirty jobs for him. Carol said this really bothered him, using his son like that. Oh yeah, Carol said that his son's name was Paco," explained Shaun.

"Shit, you got to be kidding me. Guys, this is real critical, are you sure she said Paco?"

Leon spoke first. "For sure, she said Paco at least twice."

Shaun jumped in, "Yeah, Carol said Ruhall's son's name was Paco. She said Ruhall's wife has no clue that he has a secret kid."

Both Christie and Sandy stood up and got ready to leave. "Guys, you have no way of knowing how important this information is. Please keep a lid on this, and take no further action. No phone calls, no stalking, nothing. Because of your trip we have broken the case open. This is where we have to be so careful. We must guard our information and evidence, so it will not lose its admissibility," Christie explained.

Chapter 42
Cell Site Data

SECURING A WARRANT TO access Paco Tinson's cell phone data went very smoothly. The judge who signed off on the probable cause warrant said it was not necessary, but she agreed that it was better to be safe than sorry. The rapid changes in technology had moved much faster than protections provided by the fourth amendment. Recently Congress had had bills submitted to clarify how far law enforcement could go with respect to cell site location information. One issue had to deal with real time cell site location information versus cell site data from a prior date. Christie wanted to make sure that a liberal judge did not rule that information from Paco's cell company was not admissible and jeopardize a triple murder case.

"Sandy, technology says we could have Paco's cell data by the end of the day now that Judge Cookie has signed," Christie said as they pulled onto Flower St. They were only minutes away from their meeting with Sergeant Simcic.

Mike Simcic was seated at the head of the conference room table. Detectives Morgan and Urqheart were seated on either side of him as Christie and Sandy entered the room. "Cloud, hope we did not keep you waiting?" sneered the Sargent. Before anyone could say a word, the Sergeant let it fly.

"First it appears that you two have screwed up this case from day one. Yes, I am talking to you, Cloud and you too, Anderson. I have given you every chance to close in on the drummer kid, but you guys keep chasing the ex-con from Lynnwood. Here is the deal," Sargent Simcic continued to rant. "Bobbie and Frank have determined that Forrest Dupree does not have an alibi for either his father's murder or the Flagg murder. He and his band had jobs on both nights and he had ample time to commit both killings. The motive is clear. He inherits over five million by killing his father, and by killing the Flaggs he tries to throw us off. I am going to have Morgan coordinate with our people who cover Stanton and bring him in and charge him with premeditated first degree murder. I don't know what I am going to do with you two." Simcic added.

Slowly Christie Cloud got up from her chair and went over to the large white board that covered almost a full wall. She picked up a blue erasable marker and drew a big oval on the board. Then she drew a smaller oval under the large one and connected the two with curved lines.

"Gentleman," she said with a louder than usual voice, "this is a toilet, and all three of you are about to flush your law enforcement careers down the toilet. I want you three to shut your mouth while Sandy and I try and save your careers. If you interrupt us, I will march upstairs and go directly to the Sheriff, and it is my bet that this will be your last day in uniform. A contract killer killed all the Flaggs, Steven Thigpin and Fred Dupree. A killer hired by Hal Ruhall, the owner of Ruhall Settlement Group and Zodiac Settlement Solutions, both LLCs incorporated in the state of Washington. Ruhall will collect five, four, and four million dollars. That's thirteen million dollars. Sandy and I are still tying up the case, but we are certain the Hal Ruhall hired a local ex-con by the name of Paco Tinson."

"Bullshit," shouted Simcic, "you can't tie him to this with one latent print." Simcic turned to Detective Morgan and gave him a little victory smile. Once a pig, always a pig, Christie thought.

"Sergeant, you are so correct. One latent print will not be enough, but the fact that Paco Tinson is the son of Hal Ruhall might just do the job!"

The temperature in the room dropped ten degrees. Both Sandy and Christie looked over as all the color drained out of Mike Simcic's face. He slid down in his chair and closed his eyes. For a good twenty maybe thirty seconds there was a strange silence in the conference room. Finally Simcic opened his eyes as beads of perspiration formed on his forehead. "Morgan, forget about the Dupree kid, you guys help Detectives Anderson and Cloud with anything they need to wrap this up. You two have done a wonderful job, and I am going to let upstairs know and recommend you two for a commendation. Make sure that you keep Placentia in the loop, as Thigpin is in their backyard. Again, great detective work." With that said, Sargent Simcic slowly got up from his chair and slinked out of the room.

Chapter 43
Brain Dust

PACO COULDN'T REMEMBER WHEN he did not have his nervous tics. He preferred to think of them more as a nervous affliction, he felt the word tic was gross or unclean. His mother said he might have Tourette syndrome. Sometimes he could go a full minute, other times he would be afflicted every twenty or thirty seconds. What was different with Paco's affliction was his tic was limited to the involuntary jerking of his chin to his right shoulder. He had read that as one got older, the tics would reduce in frequency and severity.

What was more of a problem was the occurrence of brain dust. At any time, Paco's thought processes would get interrupted by weird thoughts. He had always called this lack of focus his brain dust. He might be driving down the street, and would see a dog. The next thing he knew, he would start thinking about why dogs have a tail. Is the tail to swat away flies, or to swing from trees or is the dog's tail needed to wave at other dogs? This brain dust could go on for a minute or two, and he might drive past his turn or even forget where he was going.

Today, Paco was trying to focus on his current situation. For five years he was able to keep off the radar, and now he was in their crosshairs. Was he being naive to think that he was one of five suspects and the interview was just routine? He had been so careful, the dump phones, stolen cars, alibis and fake evidence that he had planted. He walked through each contract job. The Dupree case was perfect, no city cameras, a stolen car, and he even got rid of his shoes. The phony evidence had to confuse them. There was the issue of the missing envelope, but he had not licked the glue, so there can't be any DNA. Do you think that the post office keeps DNA on every envelope that is mailed? Maybe a person should use tap water to seal an envelope. He stopped himself from this episode of brain dust and tried to refocus on his problem.

With the Flagg job, he was in and out in less than a minute. He had not expected that the wife would be there, but the carb spray disabled everyone in seconds. He still hoped that the dog had not suffered.

Paco was concerned about the Thigpin hit. It was such a rush situation. He was still upset that he was not able to do his usual pre-planning. If he had made a mistake, it had to be the recent Placentia killing.

He tried to analyze the options that he had available. The first concern would his vulnerability if a search warrant was issued. He never had drugs in the house, and his computer was very clean. They could even search Google and would not find anything. That was why he did the searches prior to a hit on the search site of Ixquick. He hoped what he had read was correct, that Ixquick did not keep any IP addresses. His job at Lynnwood Parks and Rec. gave him access to the city parks, and that was where he had hidden a waterproof box of cash. When he needed to call Seattle, he would buy a new pre-paid cell from a Walgreens, use it for a couple of hours, and then destroy it.

Grab a lot of his money and hide in Mexico was always an option. Was he Hispanic or white? His mother was Hispanic, and his father was white. Barack Obama's mother was white, but his father was black. Obama implied that he was black, so what was the system? If Paco went to prison, would it be better to be Hispanic? And if he hid in Mexico, he would blend in better if he could become a Mexican.

Paco Tinson had always felt that he had a "get out of jail free card," when and how should he play it.

Yeah, his secret "get out of jail free card."

Chapter 44
Starbucks Grande

STARBUCKS WAS ITS USUAL busy self at seven thirty Tuesday morning. Christie always wanted to meet Sandy at a Starbucks, whenever possible, as she explained, "I am a long time owner of SBUX." When Christie was still working jail, a long time ago, she started buying Starbucks. She has seen her shares split three times. Christie will not tell Sandy how many shares she owns, but Christie acknowledges that it is her largest holding.

Sipping her black and bold Grande, Christie said, "Sandy we have a very busy day today, but would you say that yesterday was a red letter day?"

Sandy smiled. "Best day of my life. I heard that Simcic is out sick today."

"Sandy, we need to sort out a lot of jurisdictional issues today, but first we need to meet with Forrest. We are going to meet in Villa Park at his dad's house. Sandy, trust me on this one. I asked Lt. Genito to join us. This is a risk, but I trust him. We need someone we can trust. We can't trust the Sergeant. Are you okay with bouncing some of this stuff off of the lieutenant?"

"Christie, I am with you 100% on that, but when can I see Shaun?" Sandy interjected.

"I will set it up where Shaun can be your confidential informant," was Christie's reply.

Confidential informants were a necessary evil in the world of law enforcement. A majority of the time a C.I. was recruited during an arrest. The criminal would agree to provide information to law enforcement either for money or for a reduced charge. It was a common practice for a homicide detective to have several CIs providing them with information on criminal activity. In most cases, confidential informants were criminals or former criminals themselves.

The last two weeks have been pure hell, thought Lt. Vince Genito. He had just pulled up in front of the home of Fred Dupree and was waiting for the two homicide detectives. The pressure from the council had been relentless. It really pissed him off that there was serious talk by the city of putting out a request for proposal to the City of Anaheim and the City of Orange to take over public safety for Villa Park. Even one council member had recommended that VP get their own police department. It had been almost two decades since the Janie Pang murder. Everyone felt that the Pang case was a murder for hire. Wouldn't it be ironic if the Dupree case was also a contract hit?

Forrest pulled his Mustang into his father's driveway and was reminded of how much more work he had to do with the estate. He was wondering if he should start his dad's car, when the tall Sheriff climbed out of his SUV. "Mr. Dupree, I am Lt. Vince Genito, Chief of Public Safety here in Villa Park."

Forrest and Lt. Genito were making mostly small talk when they saw Detectives Cloud and Anderson pull up behind Genito's SUV.

After Forrest unlocked the front door, he suggested they use the dining room for their meeting. "Forrest, we have not meet before, but Detective Cloud and I were in your father's house the afternoon that your father's death was reported. Again, my condolences to you, and I understand that you have been able to add a new dimension to this case." opened Lt. Genito.

Christie spent about fifteen minutes bringing the Chief up to speed on the case. She asked Forrest to explain the life settlement business to Chief Genito. "If my father had just surrendered his policy to Victory Mutual, he would have received several hundreds of thousands of dollars less then he received by selling his policy to the Ruhall Settlement Group," explained Forrest.

"Chief, we have three murder cases in two weeks, in each case a victim had sold a large life policy to one of two companies in the life settlement business. Both of those companies are LLCs in Washington

State and both are owned by Harold Ruhall of Issaquah. We have a latent print from the scene of one victim, and that print belongs to a felon from Lynnwood by the name of Paco Tinson. Ruhall has shared with a club dancer that he has a son by the name of Paco. He told the dancer that he felt bad because he had asked him, his son Paco, to do some dirty work," explained Christie. "Lieutenant, we have several problems with this case, and we are here today to draw on your experience, because some of our challenges are political in nature," continued Christie. Christie explained to Genito the bizarre behavior that was being exhibited by the Sergeant in charge of the homicide detail. Both Sandy and Christie reviewed many of the jurisdictional challenges that these murders had created. "We could have a real bag of worms on our hands, but that is why the county pays us the big bucks. Right, Forrest?" added Chief Vince.

During the next hour the four of them prioritized the many tasks and challenges that needed to be solved to move the case along.

"It is possible that we could have a challenge from the feds that this is a RICO case," said Lt. Genito. He then continued, "Forrest, that is a racketeer influenced and corrupt organization act. The act is complicated but it allows for the leaders of a syndicate to be held accountable, in other words, to be arrested and tried, for crimes they ordered others to do for them.

"I agree with you Christie, we need more concrete evidence to link Paco to Ruhall. Once they are arrested they will lawyer up and if we are going to flip anyone we are going to need a more solid case," continued Genito. "Forrest how certain are you that the dancer, Carol Maddox, will help?" Genito asked.

"Chief, Shaun said that she was a banker for ten years before she was laid off when WaMu went down. He says she has high core values and feels that people who will not step forward cause America's problems. Christie is that what you understood?" asked Forrest.

"Yeah, she wants to make a difference, that was my read," added Christie.

"I will take this upstairs, probably talk to the Assistant Sheriff who oversees field operations and investigative services. Christie, you and Sandy meet with either the Chief or Assistant Chief at Placentia," said Lt. Genito.

"Here is where we throw the dice," volunteered Chief Genito. "If Ruhall's dancer friend can get to his wife, we might be able to solicit her help in getting some good evidence, not only on him, but maybe on the secret son, Paco."

Christie interjected a thought. "Sandy and I have interviewed Tinson twice. He knows the system. I think if we can present him with what he thinks is solid evidence, he will try and cut a deal."

Chief Genito added one more point. "Forrest, I would recommend that you have Shaun call Seattle and get a feel for how far Carol Maddox will go. Would she be willing to call Ruhall's wife and set up a meeting with her? After Shaun talks to Maddox, let me know and I will get the Chief of the Issaquah P.D. on board. Christie, you might be making a quick trip to the Pacific Northwest real soon."

Forrest locked the front door, and walked with Christie and Sandy to their car. Chief Genito had just pulled away from the curb. "Detective Cloud, if you go to Seattle, I go to Seattle," announced Forrest.

"Oh my, this is getting thick," commented Sandy as she opened the passenger door to the department's car.

Chapter 45
Carburetor Spray

THE TECHNOLOGY TEAM HAD contacted Sandy and told her that the phone company had provided the CSLI. The request for data had asked for three specific dates. Sandy thought that she would study the report and try and find any patterns before she called Christie. First she examined the data for the afternoon and night that Fred Dupree was killed. Cell site location information showed that Tinson's cell moved around the Lynnwood tower until 7:00 PM. From 7:00 PM until 1:00 AM the cell stayed with one tower in Lynnwood. During that time there were no outgoing calls and two incoming calls. The two incoming calls were from the same pre-paid.

The information from the time frame of the Flagg murders was interesting. At 7:50 PM the cell is in Lynnwood, at 8:05 and 8:11 PM, the phone is moving between cell towers near the 91 freeway in a eastern direction. At 8:14 PM the cell phone drops off of the grid. At 1:48 AM, the next morning, it is back on the grid in Lynnwood. Sandy said out load, "The SOB pulled over on the 91 east and pulled the sim card and maybe the battery from his phone."

The report from technology also showed that there was no movement and no calls in or out, during the twelve-hour of Steve Thigpin's murder.

Sandy went over the information with Christie and gave her opinion. "Sandy, I agree, real solid circumstantial. Let's get CSLI for the whole three weeks. My guess is there is only going to be three times that his phone goes off line," Christie directed. "I have another thought, remember the Flagg case, there was that issue that both husband and wife and even the dog had been sprayed, with what the lab thought was carburetor spray. I spoke to an owner of an auto repair shop and he said that carb spray is a poor man's pepper spray. He told me that if you spray a guy in the nuts, he would feel like his balls have been set on fire. He also said that a shot of the spray in the eyes would blind you for ten minutes. One more thing, carb spray comes out, not as a spray but a stream, a stream that will shoot ten feet," said Christie. "With the print, we have probable cause to get a search warrant for Tinson apartment. I am sure that there would be over spray on his clothes. What do you think?"

"My concern," said Sandy, "is he might bolt to Mexico. Let's see what happens in Seattle and whether our plan becomes a reality."

"Ok, we hold off on the apartment warrant," replied Christie.

Shaun took a big breath and dialed the number for Carol Maddox.

"This is Carol."

"Carol, this is Shaun Watanabe from California, remember the guitar guy with Purple Cinnamon?"

"Of course, how is your friend Leon, and more importantly your friend whose father was killed?"

Shaun explained to Carol a little about the progress, and asked if she was still willing to help with the case.

"Shaun, let me be clear, my first priority is my child, then I want to make a difference. Nobody has the guts to step forward. Radical Islam has declared war on America, Shaun, and nobody has the nerve to talk about it. Tell me how I can help catch that bastard, and I will do it."

Carol listened as Shaun explained how the police needed her to call Maureen Ruhall. "Tell her that you have been a friend of her husband's for the last six months, and that you have information, confidential information, that she as Hal's wife should have. You might also say, that if she is curious about where her husband has been going all these evenings, she should meet you for coffee. Recommend a Starbucks in the middle of the day, so she will not be fearful. Try and set it up, not tomorrow, but the next day, so we can have time to fly up."

Shaun and Carol talked for another half an hour. He was shocked that she expressed no call reluctance or fear of making the call.

Christie had a successful trip to the Placentia PD. She had been to their PD a couple of times and she remembered the terrible tragedy when their Sargent Gene Stuckenschneider Jr. was killed on a highway changing a tire. Not only did Christie attend the funeral service, but she also returned when the City of Placentia planted a special tree and bench at the station in memory of Big Gene the Mean Machine.

Her meeting with the Chief and Deputy Chief went very well. The detectives provided her with the contents of their case file on Thigpin. Both the Chief and Deputy Chief seemed to have above average business experience, because they grasped the concepts of life insurance and life settlement issues very quickly. They were okay with letting the OCSD deal with the departments of insurance in California and Washington. The Deputy Chief was concerned that the insurance companies might pay the claim while their agencies tried to develop a solid case. Christie explained that she has been in contact with the claims department of both companies.

Forrest felt that it had been a good day. He was feeling a victory, because he had just spent over three hours organizing his father's paperwork. His father's accounts that were set up in the Dupree Family Trust were the easiest to move into his own name. He found a few accounts that were in his father's name and not the trust—those would take a little more time—but the attorney who had helped his father set up the trust was still in business. Because of FDIC limits, Forrest took the time to set up savings and checking accounts at several different banks. For the first time since his dad's death, he allowed his mind to consider the impact of now having over five million dollars. He concluded that he was going to become very astute with his finances. Forrest had read that the majority of people who come into large amount of money were broke and miserable in a short period of time; he was determined to be neither.

The issue of his father's house was in his thoughts when his cell phone rang. "Detective Cloud," Forrest said with amusement.

Christie told Forrest about her meeting at the Placentia PD, and also told him, in confidence, about the cell site location data. "I am sure that when we get the rest of Tinson's phone info, we are going to see that his pattern of usage was consistent except when he was out committing a major crime. That is good news, but I will celebrate when we get some hard evidence, stuff that is not circumstantial," Christie shared.

"Christie, good news, I am getting a call from Shaun, maybe he got a call back from Carol Maddox, I'll take it and call you right back."

Chapter 46
Call From a Stripper

MAUREEN HAD STARTED ASSEMBLING some clothes for her annual overnight with her sister. Tomorrow, her sister and she would meet at Seattle's Four Seasons Hotel and attend a play and have an upscale dinner. They always booked a pair of Deluxe Elliot Bay Suites. She was looking forward to some time with her best friend. Her sister was the one person that she could confide in about her marriage and her challenges of living with Hal. Maureen thoughts were a million miles away when the ringing of her phone startled her.

"Maureen my name is Carol Maddox, I know your husband Hal very well, and I would hope that you would listen to my story. Do you have a few minutes Mrs. Ruhall?"

"Who are you again?" Maureen asked. Maureen's mind was racing, should she hang up? Maybe this was a joke, Maureen had thought she had seen and heard it all, what the heck, she decided to go for it.

"My name is Carol and I live in Lake City. Mrs. Ruhall, I have known your husband for about six months and I have some information that I feel is critical that you have. My only purpose is to meet you this week for coffee, no more than ten minutes. Maureen, I assure you this call is legit. I would assume you have been wondering where you husband goes, when he says he is going to work in the evening so often."

"Are you having an affair with my husband?" Maureen asked. "Mrs.

Ruhall, I was an exotic dancer, I have never seen or been with your husband outside of the club where I worked. I can promise you that the information I want to share will be extremely valuable. Please trust me. Can we meet at a coffee shop during the day in the next day or so?"

Maureen almost felt faint. She was not upset and she was not scared. She pushed some of her clothes aside and set down on the bed. "Mrs. Maddox, are you pregnant?" she realized that that was a stupid question, but she did not know what else to ask. "No, and as I said, I want no money. I danced naked at a gentleman's club for your husband and he told me some things you will want to know."

Maureen told Carol that she was going to be out of town the next day, and they agreed to meet Friday at the Starbucks that was inside the Fred Meyer store in Issaquah. The time was set for 10:30 AM.

She had to tell her sister. Maureen kept nothing from her. Actually she was feeling a bit of excitement. She knew that her relationship with Hal was all screwed up, maybe this meeting with the stripper would bring the situation to a head. "Monica, you better sit down, after we do the town tomorrow, I am going to have a secret meeting with a stripper."

"Forrest, we are a go, Carol has set up a meeting with Maureen Ruhall at a Starbucks at 10:30 AM this Friday. Oh, the Starbucks is in Issaquah, I can show you and Christie the bronze salmon and we can drink at the Issaquah Brew House. I am so psyched," bantered Shaun.

Chapter 47
Conference Room, Homicide Unit

THE CONFERENCE ROOM IN the homicide unit was in operation early Wednesday morning. Coffee cups, bagels and file folders were covering the table. Unlike a corporate boardroom with the traditional big shiny walnut table, this table was made of four Formica steel-legged tables pushed together. Lt. Vince Genito and the Orange County District Attorney's office had been in constant communication. The Ruhall case, as it was now referred to, was pushed to the top of the OCDA's executive team. This morning, Marc Innis was in attendance for the Ruhall strategy session. Marc had been practicing law for over twenty-five years. After graduating from the famous Yale Law School, he entered private practice, and after six years, he was recruited by the District Attorney to join the team at the Orange County District Attorney's office. Now Marc Innis was the Senior Assistant District Attorney in charge of the Vertical Prosecution/Violent Crimes Division. Murder and elder abuse were part of his unit's focus.

Joining Lt. Vince Genito and Marc Innis were Christie, Sandy, Bobbie and Frank. Bobbie Morgan and Frank Urqheart had been busy getting hard copies of forms, applications and memos that pertained to Steven Thigpin selling his policy to Zodiac Settlement Solutions, LLC. They also had downloaded the certificate of formation from The State of Washington Secretary of State, that provided the UBI Number and the consent to serve as registered agent. Their documents showed that Harold L. Ruhall was the registered agent for both LLCs.

Lt. Genito was the first to speak. "This morning I met with Assistant Sheriff Benedict, and during the meeting, Sheriff Campbell stuck her head in. As we expected everyone upstairs is now onboard. A.S. Benedict spoke with the Justice Department. He said that they will respect our jurisdiction, but once we make our arrests, they will do an evaluation of the applicability of R.I.C.O. Marc Innis said that the DA was on board, he just wants to be kept in the loop. "If this breaks in our favor, he needs to be a part of any press conferences." added Marc.

Sandy gave everyone a copy of the two tech reports from the phone companies' cell site location information. "Who ordered the warrant before the CSLI request went to phone company?" the assistant D.A. asked.

"I did," replied Christie.

"Brilliant move, not needed currently, but I am a member of a working committee that is trying to predict the direction of the 9th Circuit and Congress. Thanks Christie," explained the Special Assistant District Attorney. The team examined the three weeks of cell activity. The dormant times and the times the phone went off line all matched the three murders. "I am willing to go to trial with the fingerprint and this cell data. However ,we hold off until the Seattle trip. I want the big guy. I want Ruhall," Marc repeated.

Bobbie Morgan provided the results of their investigation of the four guys that Tinson had put down as his poker alibi. "Two of the guys are totally off the radar, but the other two are in the system. Here are their rap sheets, and here is Tinson's. Tinson has been clean for three years and it has been five since a conviction. All three have the same ink, FTC. The tattoo FTC doesn't come up on our gang tattoo software and the twenty plus Lynnwood gangs don't match FTC in ether English or Spanish," explained Morgan.

Everyone agreed to keep a soft touch on Tinson and his buddies for a few days. "I bet he bolts south as soon as he smells serious heat," said Sandy.

Frank Urqheart had been unusually quiet during the meeting. As the meeting started to wind up he asked Lt. Genito the whereabouts of Sergeant Simcic. Vince Genito answered his question by saying that he was out for a couple of days on PTO. Christie looked at Sandy, lowered her head slightly, and raised her eyebrows as if to say, bullshit, he is afraid to come in because he is embarrassed for being so wrong.

"Christie," Lt Genito said, "We need Shaun Watanabe in Seattle because he has the relationship now with Maddox the dancer banker. I guess I am ok with Forrest, because Shaun insists, but keep him on a short leash. He is traveling with you, but he is without portfolio."

Sandy asked the Chief, "What is 'without portfolio?'"

"That means he is unofficial, not authorized and most important, we have no liability," explained Genito.

Christie and Sandy stuck around to clean up the room. Marc, from OCDA's office, stuck his head back into the conference room and said, "Detectives, very nice work."

Chapter 48
Tacoma, Washington

PARTY LIGHTS IN SEATTLE, thought Sandy. She would have loved to have been able to join Christie, Forest and Shaun on the Seattle trip. It was business, but she would have had fun and she liked the lead guitar of Purple Cinnamon. But the team needed her to keep things from unraveling at the station. Sandy also recognized that she was not a fan of commercial airlines. Her sister had been as a flight attendant for fifteen years, and had shared with Sandy too many stories about the food, water and close calls. Sandy had heard enough that she tried to avoid flying. The Sheriff's department helicopter was another story. Sandy had flown three times with the department, and loved it. The Ruhall case was generating a large pile of paperwork, and Sandy figured she should make a big dent in it while Christie was gone.

Lt. Genito volunteered to drop the group of at the Orange County Airport. As the three pilled out of the Chief's SUV, the Lt. hollered at Christie. "Detective, you got your ok to carry letter from the Sheriff?"

"Yes, ready to rock and roll with the TSA." Christie replied.

Needless to say, the rules about bringing firearms on board commercial airlines had been significantly changed since 9/11. H.R. 218 was a new Federal law that protected law enforcement officers from all the different state and local rules with regards to carrying concealed firearms. The problem was that it was a rare event when TSA and the various airlines are on the same page.

The system seemed to work for Christie on this flight, She gave the Alaska ticket agent her permission to carry letter plus her sheriff department identification. In return, the Alaska counter agent gave Christie paperwork in triplicate for TSA, and to give to the boarding flight attendant.

The TSA line was short and both Shaun and Forrest were able to avoid tripping the beep beep machine. Christie went through a different line, where she was escorted to a private area and cleared by TSA even before Forrest and Shaun. Today Christie was wearing a navy blue pantsuit that did a good job of concealing her Glock.

Detective Cloud was called out for early boarding because she had declared that she was carrying her firearm. She gave the ticket agent a copy of her paper work and then was introduced to the flight crew. The Alaska Air Captain noted her seat and told her that he was also certified to carry and today was armed. She then went to her seat and waited for Forrest and Shaun to board.

Alaska Flight 503 was on schedule to land in Seattle before three o'clock. Christie felt that there was so much at stake tomorrow, that she could not afford a delayed or cancelled flight, so the decision was made to travel a day early.

The flight went smoothly and the two-hour-plus time went by very quickly with the first hour taken up by a discussion of collegiate track and field. Forrest was intrigued by Christie's knowledge of kinesiology and her technique to throw the javelin fifty-three meters.

"We have the afternoon and evening open, guys, any suggestions before we meet up with the Issaquah P.D. in the morning?" Christie asked.

"I hope that you two let me buy you the best hamburger in the world. All of my life, my dad told me that he grew up on Frisko Freeze double cheeseburgers. In honor of my father, let's make a trip to Tacoma."

Forrest drove South on I-5, while Shaun acted as navigator. During the drive to Tacoma, Christie checked in with Sandy, as she was curious as to whether Sergeant Simcic had made his arrival. "Guys, Sandy says no news is good news, very quiet in Orange County."

As the threesome continued south, Shaun pointed out the pastel painted Tacoma Dome and the famous LeMay Auto collection. Shaun relished the thought that he was the man of wisdom and knowledge and with this in mind, he did another search on his iPad. "Here is the scoop; Harold LeMay made a fortune in the garbage business, started collecting cars, and according to the Internet, he had 3,500 cars in the 90's. This new museum will hold up to 500 cars, trucks and motorcycles."

Christie jumped in, "OK, Shaun, if you had 3,500 cars and you washed them every two weeks, how many cars did Mr. LeMay wash every day?"

Forrest was trying to figure out how to merge over to Highway 16, but he interjected, "the answer is Mr. Lemay did not wash any of his 3,500 cars. The garbage truck drivers came in on the weekends and did the car washes."

Shaun could not resist. "1750 cars a week, five days a week, equals 350 cars to wash a day."

Hal Ruhall hung up the phone after another futile effort to get Victory Mutual to process the two death claims. Once insurance company has a copy of the death certificate and other required forms, they will usually pay out the policies death benefit within five to ten days. Hal knew that a death claim would be sent to a claims specialist, but what he didn't know was that both Detective Cloud and now Lt Genito had been in daily communication with both Victory Mutual and Mutual of New England.

"Three double cheeseburgers, two fries, chocolate shake and two diet colas," ordered Forrest from the little window off of the small parking lot. Forrest wondered how many times his father and mother had stood in this same spot while ordering Frisko Freeze burgers. His father even had a picture of the famous Frisko Freeze sign that was visible from Division Ave. The big red sign, white letters and big white curved arrow had been a part of Tacoma's landscape ever since gas company driver Perry Smith opened the burger joint in 1951. Forrest was raised on stories by his father about how all the teenagers would drive between Frisko Freeze, Bush's drive-in and the Cloverleaf Tavern. During the fifties and sixties, Division Ave and 6th Ave was a constant parade of sports cars, muscle cars and the family ride. As Forrest drove west on 6th Ave., Shaun placed a call to Carol Maddox.

"Shaun, you wouldn't believe it, Ruhall's wife, Maureen called to confirm that I was going to be at Starbucks in the morning. It looks like we are all set," explained Carol. Shaun went on to explain that he and

Forrest were in Tacoma along with the lead detective on the case. They agreed on the time and place for their morning rendezvous.

"Guys, we have two more places to check out, then we can head back to Seattle. The next part of the tour is for the benefit of Christie." said Forrest as he turned from 6th Ave down Union Ave.

"This is the University of Puget Sound, our celebrity attended this University for about a year." Turning left on 26th, Forrest then drove past Mason Junior High. "He or she attended Mason for three years. After driving down Stevens St., Forrest announced that the mystery person attended Jefferson Elementary School."

"Forrest, goddamnit, who are we talking about?" laughed Christie.

"You'll get your answer in five minutes," Forrest answered as he drove back toward 6th Ave. "On your right is Wilson High School. Our celebrity attended Wilson and graduated in 1965."

"Okay, here you are," said Forrest as he pulled the rental up to a small home on Skyline Drive. "Lady and gentleman, you have seen one of the Universities that he attended, his elementary school, junior high, and high school. This is the home he lived in while living in Tacoma. This is the Tacoma home of Theodore Bundy."

"My god," shouted Christie, "this is so cool. Forrest, you do not understand what this means. Bundy stuff comes up all in my work. To be a able to tell my associates that I have been to Bundy's schools and house is over the top. Forrest you are the best," Christie said as she leaned over and gave him a little kiss on the cheek.

Chapter 49
Galloping Gertie

MAUREEN AND HER SISTER Monica had a great time on their "Sisters Do Seattle" trip. The Four Sessions was superb, as was their two-hour dinner at the El Gaucho. The only thing that outdid Maureen's Anderson Ranch Natural Rack of Lamb were the two bottles of 2008 Cadence Camerata Red Mountain.

"Maureen, are you having any second thoughts about meeting with Hal's stripper tomorrow?" asked her sister Monica.

"No and I actually just called her, her name is Carol, and we just confirmed the coffee meeting." replied Maureen.

"Sis, you are brave, and I think you are doing the right thing. Are you sure that you don't want me to join you?" As Maureen and her sister gossiped about the possible outcomes, Maureen felt certain that she was doing what was best.

"Shaun, bring up a YouTube of Galloping Gertie and show Christie where we are going." For six minutes, Christie watched the famous Tacoma Narrows Bridge and its historic collapse just four months after it opened on July 1 1940. The three drove over the westbound bridge and took Exit 10, circled around and returned going east on Highway 16. They stopped at the toll and crossed the 5,400 feet of the new eastbound bridge. Forrest explained that after the bridge collapsed in 1940, it took ten years to build the 1950 Narrows Bridge. The 1940 and 1950 bridges were the third longest suspension bridges in the world.

"Ok, we're going to stay on the 16 and then merge to I-5 north and head to Seattle," announced Forest.

Shaun referred to his iPad as they drove by Tacoma's minor league baseball stadium, home to the Tacoma Rainiers. Shaun announced, "the ballpark is called Cheney Stadium. It is now the home of the Seattle Mariners Triple A minor league team and when it opened in 1960, it was the Triple A club for the San Francisco Giants." Shaun spent the next fifteen minutes reviewing all of the major league players who passed through Tacoma's team.

Lt. Genito called Christie for an update and was pleased that Friday's meeting with Ruhall's wife was still on track. Christie then inquired about how the surveillance was going with Paco Tinson. "We have Tinson under a light touch, we don't want him to feel any heat and bolt to Mexico. L.A. Sheriff's department says he is coming to work each day and appears normal." explained Genito. He also let Christie know that the Issaquah P.D. was on board and that they were expecting them to drop by in the morning before the Starbucks interview.

"We need to discuss some important stuff, before we have drinks at the Keg Steakhouse. Forrest, you were a great tour guide, but you missed one important Tacoma celebrity. We drove by Jefferson and Mason schools, but not only did Bundy go there, but rock and roll legend Rockin' Robin Roberts also went to those schools," Shaun said enthusiastically.

"Who is Rockin' Robin Roberts?" inquired Christie.

Shaun jumped at the opportunity to expound on his vast knowledge of rock-in-roll history. "Robin is considered the musician who put 'Louie Louie' on the map. In the mid-fifties he was singing on a bench at the Puyallup Fair when two other musicians discovered him. They formed a band called the Blue Notes. Richard Berry had written 'Louie Louie' in Southern California. The song was fairly dormant but Robin Roberts found a copy and fell in love with it. He then left the Blue Notes and became a member of Tacoma's local rock band Wailers. Roberts added 'Louie' to the Wailers song book and the rest is history. The Fabulous Wailers performed 'Louie' for several years while doing Northwest gigs. A Portland band called The Kingsmen recorded the song in 1963 and it went national. Here is the sad part of the 'Louie' story. Rockin' Robin Roberts was working on an advanced degree in Biochemistry and was killed in a auto accident in 1967. The Wailers version of 'Louie Louie' was the best because of the high voice *let's give it to em right now* lyrics that Roberts would scream during their version."

"Shaun, I must say that I will never be able hear 'Louie Louie' without remembering this day trip to Tacoma." said Christie. The three had finished their burgers and were relaxed and quiet for the rest of the trip to the Silver Cloud Inn.

"Let's check in and relax for a hour or two and then we can go over to the Keg for dinner and some drinks," announced Forrest.

"That's perfect, I need to check in with Sandy and Chief Genito and make sure that Tinson has not made a run to Mexico," replied Christie.

"I will have the Zesty Salmon." Christie told the waiter. The waiter then took the orders of Forrest and Shaun. They were still working on their starters, an order of crab, parmesan and spinach dip and a order of scallops and bacon. Forrest had chosen the blue cheese fillet and Shaun went for the prime rib and tiger shrimp. The waiter had delivered Christie a glass of Chateau Ste. Michelle 2009 Sauvignon Blanc Horse Heaven Hills, Shaun had a pint of Hales Nut Brown Ale, Forrest had a Keg sized Cadillac Margarita.

"Forrest, I hope this is appropriate to say, but you know that your father was drinking a Cadillac Margarita the night he died?" said Christie.

"Yes, thank you. You reminded me that he always put a little Patron topper and he would announce to whoever was with him; for ten percent more, you go first class." With that said, Forrest ordered a side shot of Patron Silver. Two hours later, Forrest, Shaun and Detective Cloud drove the short distance back to the Silver Cloud Inn. The complementary wine bar had been closed for hours, so Christie got off on the second floor and Forrest and Shaun continued up to the third floor.

After three rings Forrest answered the room's phone, "Forrest, I couldn't sleep. I am down in the lobby lounge having tea, do you want to join me?"

Chapter 50
Gilda and Finley

"You always want to do an advance recon of the site where you are going to conduct an operation. The objective is to minimize surprises and knowing the territory will give us a psychological advantage." Christie explained. They each ordered a Starbucks and headed over to the Issaquah Police Department for the 9:00 a.m. introduction and planning meeting with the Chief.

"The P.D. is only ten minutes away. It is over on Sunset Way. We have time to swing by the Salmon Hatchery so you two can see Gilda and Finley," announced Shaun.

"Who is Gilda, another stripper? asked Christie.

"Be patient, trust me, this will only take five minutes," said Shaun as he directed Forrest to the hatchery.

"See—Gilda and Finley." explained Shaun. "Aren't they cool, made out of bronze. The plaque says this is what a salmon looked like five million years ago." Five minutes later they were on their way to 130 East Sunset Way.

The police department was housed in a relatively new building that also housed city hall. The Chief met them and brought them back to his office. "We have a department of fifty, and Issaquah has thirty thousand residents and another ten thousand come in during the day. Our violent crime is below average and non-violent property theft is above average. We have more auto thefts, larceny and arson then we should. Washington has more than its share of meth users and labs than the average state." explained the Chief. He then introduced them to Detective Moran, who would join them at the Fred Meyer store.

The five spent another thirty minutes discussing the case and the strategy not only with respect to the meeting with Maureen Ruhall, but the timing of both a California and Issaquah arrest. Their concern was, when Ruhall is picked up, he would lawyer up fast and might get the word to Tinson in L.A. Everyone agree, that Mrs. Ruhall's cooperation would give the case a new direction. If she cooperated, any evidence that she provided would be admissible.

The Issaquah police chief mentioned that he had had a conversation with Lt. Genito about husband-wife privilege as it related to the admissibility of evidence. Communication between a husband and wife is usually considered privileged and would not normally be admissible. In addition, a spouse could not be compelled to testify against their spouse, but they could volunteer to testify so long as the testimony was not a privileged conversation. "Fruit from the poison tree" was the doctrine that said that a chain of evidence that originated from illegally obtained evidence was also inadmissible.

Maureen felt unusually calm that morning, considering the drama that the day promised. Hal seemed his normal self, and Maureen made small talk about all the errands that she was going to have to run. Before he headed to his car, Hal mentioned that Saturday night would be a great time to go out for a nice dinner. "Sounds good to me, so long as we can go some place that has good wine," Maureen said laughingly.

Carol Maddox drove her four-year-old Infiniti down East Lake Sammamish Parkway until she saw the turn into the Fred Meyer store. It was 9:30 and she was going to meet Shaun and the cop from Southern California, but she first needed to locate the store's restroom.

The plan was to avoid overwhelming Carol, so it was agreed that Shaun and Christie would initially meet her, while Forrest and Detective Moran would hang back in the shadows.

"Gigi, Shaun Watanabe. Good to see you again, and let me introduce Detective Christie Cloud," said Shaun as he stood up as Carol walked up to the small Starbucks counter. Christie was prepared for a big girl, but she did not realize that the exotic dancer would also be six feet tall.

"Detective, please call me Carol, Gigi is from a prior life," she laughed. "Shaun you said the drummer was going to fly up with you?" asked Carol.

"He is over there by the sushi counter with a detective from the Issaquah P.D." replied Shaun.

"Carol we wanted to keep a low profile and also did not want Mrs. Ruhall to feel crowded or under pressure." added Christie. After ordering an assortment of Starbucks coffees, Christie led the conversation as to what they hoped to be able to accomplish.

"Carol, I will sit here with you for the meeting. Shaun, Forrest and the Issaquah detective will give us space, but be close by. Our primary objective is to convince Mrs. Ruhall to provide us with some information or evidence that will help us connect her husband with Paco Tinson. I suggest that you start slowly, first explain the relationship you had with Ruhall, and then ask her permission for me to enter the conversation. This is going to be hard because we are going to be hitting her with some pretty heavy stuff all at once." explained Christie.

"Monica, I think I should have hammered back a couple of Bloody Mary's this morning," Maureen told her sister while parked at the Issaquah Fred Meyer.

"Sis, you are brave, but I agree with you, but this is something that you need to do, something is going on with Hal, and you deserve to know what's up."

"I will call you as soon as I can, wish me luck." Carol closed her cell, grabbed her purse and walked into the Fred Meyer store.

Chapter 51
Maureen Ruhall

CHRISTIE WAS THE FIRST to spot Mrs. Ruhall. Years of police work provided a good cop with special powers of observation and Christie sensed that the attractive woman approaching the coffee stand displayed typical signs of preoccupation and nervousness. "Carol, the lady with the blue Nordstrom blazer looks like a good fit."

Carol got up from her coffee bar stool and made her approach.

"Mrs. Ruhall?" Carol quietly asked.

"Yes, and you then are Carol Maddox." replied Maureen.

"Since I called you, let me get your coffee. I already have one going, what can I get you?"

"Straight scotch," said Maureen breaking the awkwardness of the moment. "Grande black coffee will be fine, and thank you."

With coffee in hand, Maureen walked with Carol back to the table and pulled up a chair while looking at Christie and wondering if she was with Carol.

"Maureen, I hope you do not mind, but I asked Detective Cloud to join us. I think you will like her and I feel that she will be able to help us."

"Help us with what?" asked Maureen with a lot of nervousness in her voice.

"Mrs. Ruhall, my name Christie Cloud. I am a detective with the Orange County Sheriff's Department in Southern California, but I hope you will please call me Christie." With a sincere smile on her face, Christie extended her hand to Maureen.

"Christie very nice to meet you, but please excuse me, I am so nervous I am afraid I might pee my pants. I have a million emotions going through me right now."

Christie jumped in, "Carol, why don't you explain to Maureen why we wanted to meet her and why I am up from California?"

"As I explained on the phone, until last week, I spent six months dancing naked at a joint called the Lotus Girl in Lake City. I know I am big, but in the exotic dancing business, a girl like me can be very popular. Your husband Hal knew me as Gigi, and he would asked for me when he came in."

"I don't believe this, Why would that jerk drive to Lake City? How often did he come in?" asked Maureen.

"I am sorry Maureen. It would be natural for you to hate me."

"Carol, I do not blame you. Maybe I am to blame," said Maureen as she reached into her purse for a piece of tissue.

"Your husband came in once or twice a week for the last five months. We have a couple of private rooms that are called VIP rooms. They are five hundred dollars an hour, and we would always go to a VIP room and I would dance for him. I hope you believe me, when I tell you that these club have video cameras everywhere, and all I ever did was dance."

Carol continued to explain to Maureen the dynamics between her and Hal. She told her about Hal's name Frankel, and his childhood experience with voyeurism and his fetish for women with enormous breasts.

"Maureen, are you ok? I have some additional things, and you might want to be prepared."

"Go for it, I am pissed, and I am also embarrassed that my husband cannot find satisfaction at home. That bastard has been spending a thousand a month, hell two thousand a month, and he told me he was at the office. What else can you tell me, and when are you going to tell me why a California detective is here?"

"A week or so back, your husband came to the club and told me that he has been keeping a secret from you for over twenty-five years. Hal told me that, I am sorry Maureen, that he has a family, that he has a son living in Los Angeles."

"Bullshit, I cannot have children, you are wrong." Maureen responded as she wiped her eyes.

Carol continued, "He told me he had a one night stand a long time ago, and that affair resulted in a son, a son by the name of Paco."

Carol felt a slight wave of nausea pass over her as a million thoughts entered her mind. Her first thought went to denial, and in a second or two she was feeling anger. In those two seconds, she processed thousands of conversations, observations and feelings. The name Paco helped fill in a couple of old mysteries that she had been carrying for many years. About seven to ten years ago, she had received a collect call from the California department of corrections—the operator said the call was from Paco. It was during the day and Hal was still at work. She told the operator that the call was a mistake and did not accept the call. Another time, a five thousand dollar check was returned from a Los Angeles address because water had smeared the address on the envelope. Hal had explained it away, saying that it was a charitable donation required for a business transaction.

"Ladies, part of me says to get up and forget this meeting ever happened. Another part of me says stay. I am in, what else do you have?" Christie seemed to notice a change in Maureen's demeanor, she seemed to transition from emotion and humiliation to anger and determination. Christie gave Carol a little nudge under the table signaling that she was going to pick up the conversation.

"Maureen, before I explain my role, can we get you anything, are you doing okay?"

"Thank you. No I am not okay, but I can hang in here. I want to hear it all, don't hold back, I want it all," said Maureen with a newfound strength and curiosity.

Christie then inquired, "Carol just told you that your husband has a son in California. What are you thinking?"

Maureen took a deep breath, reached for a sip of her coffee, and explained that it was a possibility. Maureen told Christie and Carol that their marriage had been on autopilot for many years, and ever since Hal had retired from Northeastern Surety Life, he had seemed to be a different person. "Yes, Christie, it certainly is possible that Hal could have a son."

"Maureen, what do you know of your husband's business?" Christie asked in a casual manner. This was a key moment, and Christie was looking for any sign that Mrs. Ruhall might push back. I knew a lot more about his career at Northeastern, than I do about his settlement business. I do know that he borrowed a ton of money and liquidated our large 401K so he could buy up in-force policies. I have overheard him tell some investors that there have been problems with the calculations used to determine how much to pay a person for their policy.

Maureen continued, "I did hear that two of his policies just matured and the company will be getting some large checks soon from the insurance companies."

"Mrs. Ruhall, you have been very patient, and you have been given a lot of very disturbing news this morning. If you are up to it, I would like to introduce you to another person. Are you sure you are okay?" questioned Christie.

"I am fine, I told you, don't hold back. Look, you guys have turned my world upside down, but I want all the truth."

Christie got up from her stool and walked over to Forrest and Detective Moran. After a few moments the three of them walked together back over to the Starbucks table.

"Mrs. Ruhall, my name is Forrest Dupree."

Chapter 52
Ruhall's Home

"Mrs. Ruhall, I live in Southern California and my father had a large life insurance policy that he felt he no longer needed. Several years ago he sold the policy to Ruhall Settlement Group, LLC. I understand that your husband owns Ruhall Settlement Group. Two weeks ago my father was murdered in the doorstep of his home," Forrest said with the upmost sincerity.

"Mrs. Ruhall," said Christie, "a week later another person who had sold their policy to your husband was also murdered."

Maureen seemed a little puzzled. "What would this have to do with my husband? He has not been to California. You are not suggesting that Hal had anything to do with a murder?"

There was a solid minute or two and no one said anything. Christie held back, and let Maureen process what she had been told. It seemed to Christie that Maureen was very bright and she was betting that she would connect the dots.

Christie felt the time was right. "Maureen, we have evidence that your husband's son, Paco, was involved in the death of this man's father. The two policies that you said were maturing were not maturing. The insured's on both of those policies were murdered within a week." Christie reached across the table and took Maureen's hand in her hands. "Maureen, will you help us bring the killer of Forrest father to justice?"

Maureen looked around the table, and while still having her hand held by Detective Cloud, and with tears pouring down her checks, she said, "if that bastard of a husband of mine has done what you are suggesting, you have any help I can give."

Christie got up from the table and went over to Maureen's side. "Let's take a break, I will walk you to the restroom—if you don't mind being seen with a cop."

Maureen did not answer; she just reached out for Christie and gave her a big hug. Nobody noticed, but Forrest had tears in his eyes.

"Guys, I must get back to work. I am back in the banking business. My depositors at the branch do not need to know about Gigi and the Lotus Club." Shaun and Forrest thanked Carol and promised that they would pass Carol's hello along to Leon.

While Christie and Maureen were in the ladies' room, Detective Moran picked up another round of coffee. Moran had to admit to himself that this chick cop from So Cal had played Ruhall's wife like a Stradivarius violin. He also enjoyed the half hour he spent with Forrest and Shaun, and he had to complement Forrest for yesterdays Tacoma trip and the legacy of Ted Bundy. The detective reminded Forrest and Shaun that before The Fabulous Wailers covered "Louie Louie," they had hit a home run with the instrumental "Tall Cool One."

Mrs. Ruhall looked a lot more composed as she and Christie returned to the table. Detective Moran restarted the conversation, "Mrs. Ruhall, I just spoke with Chief Scioscia, and he extends his concern and wants you to know that you are in his prayers."

"I have met the Chief at several fundraisers and I think he is a nice man. He also has a great wife—you know she is a good artist," added Maureen.

"Mrs. Ruhall, I want you to understand that you do not have to help us. The law is very clear that you cannot be forced to testify against your husband, and that conversations between spouses are typically not considered as admissible evidence. If you want to help us, then that is considered as admissible to a jury."

"Mr. Moran, what did I say? I will help you any way I can."

For the next ten minutes Christie and Detective Moran analyzed their options. They then placed a call to Chief Scioscia. It was agreed that Detective Cloud, Forrest, and Shaun would get some lunch at the Issaquah Brewery and then meet at the police station. Maureen would drive home and Detective Moran would follow her in an unmarked car.

If Hal Ruhall's car were home then they would go to the courthouse and get a warrant. If the coast were clear, then Moran and Mrs. Ruhall would look around the family office.

Fifteen minutes had passed and the Issaquah detective was still searching through the files on the Ruhall family computer. Moran had not found any incriminating files, but he did find a few emails that had been forwarded from Ruhall Settlement Group. The detective then found an email account that was set up with Gmail. Moran went to search, and selected addressee, subject, and content and entered the name Paco.

Bingo! "Mrs. Ruhall will you come here please?" Detective Moran then said, "Only with your permission, but I would like to copy these three emails onto this thumb drive I brought."

Maureen replied, "With pleasure, yes, you have my permission." She walked out of the room with a smug smile on her face.

Maureen then picked up the handset to the house phone and called her sister. "Sis, how would you like a houseguest tonight?"

Chapter 53
Chief Scioscia

"Two Portland State IPAs, and one black and bitter coffee," Shaun told the bartender at the Issaquah Brewhouse. "Christie, we're celebrating, let me buy you a Rogue beer?"

"Last night, I locked my piece up in my room, today it is in my purse. When I carry, no booze." explained Christie. "Forrest, when I am at home I lock up my weapons, if you know what I mean." Christie said as she let her leg make solid contact with Forest.

"Loud and clear detective." replied Forrest as he felt a surge of blood light up his junk.

After their fast lunch, Christie, Shaun and Forrest drove back to the Issaquah station.

Chief Scioscia was having fun reminiscing with Forrest and Shaun about the influence of Northwest Rock n' Roll. The Chief said he still had some old 45's that the Ventures put out in the early 60's. "I still have two copies of 'Walk, Don't Run.'"

Detective Moran made a courtesy knock on the Chief's door and walked in. He had a thumb drive inside a properly labeled evidence bag. "Chief, we have got an email from Ruhall to another email account. Inside the content it says, *Paco, package on the way. Share with your mother.* Chief, we certainly have probable cause to pull a warrant for home and office, and I think we can execute an arrest warrant."

"Moran, if you found this email in fifteen minutes, think what we can find if we had his office computer and files for a week." replied the Chief. "Detective Cloud, you are the lead on this case, and from what I have seen and heard, your performance and execution has been superb," said the Chief. "And before I forget, we usually discourage civilians from getting too involved in an active case, but Mr. Dupree, you and your posse—let's see, oh yeah, Purple Cinnamon—have added a unique dimension to this case. Nice job. Now stay out of Issaquah, unless you are in town for a gig.

"Christie, let me throw out an idea. Ruhall is going to go home tonight and his wife is not going to be home. God knows what he will do, he may call California, call his sister in-law, who knows. Christie, I think you should call Genito and if they have not already done so, get the warrant process started. Issaquah and O.C. Sheriff and our appropriate D.A.s coordinate tonight an arrest on both Ruhall and your guy Tinson. You guys take the next plane home, and that way you will be home to be involved in the charging and interrogation of Tinson tomorrow."

"Chief, I agree. My biggest concern is that Tinson gets a tip or feels the heat and makes a border run. Yes, if it is okay with you, I would love it if Issaquah could hook-up Ruhall before he can tip off his son. Let's call Lt. Genito and see if he can get the ball started and get Paco Tinson in lock-up tonight." said Christie as she nodded agreement with Chief Scioscia and Detective Moran.

Lt. Genito was just about to call Christie, when his desk phone rang. Chief Scioscia had moved the group into the conference room and was using a Polycom conference table phone. "Chief, Christie, I am here with Chief Scioscia, half of our favorite band, and Detective Moran. Do you think the DA's office can get us a set of warrants, so we can move on Tinson today?"

The conference call lasted a little less than a half an hour. They reviewed the success of the meeting with Maureen Ruhall, Detective Moran's download of the Paco emails and the concern that Ruhall would trip out when he discovered his wife had left the home. Genito promised Christie they would keep Sergeant Simcic away from Tinson and let her have first shot at him in the morning. Both Scioscia and Genito felt their people could secure warrants in time so that they could make the arrest of Ruhall and Tinson between 5 and 6 PM. The call ended after Christie agreed to call Vince Genito as soon as she landed in Orange County.

Alaska flight 516 was scheduled to depart Seattle at 6:32 p.m. and would arrive in John Wayne about 9:00 p.m. Christie was the wheel person and Forrest was using Shaun's iPad to make the flight arrangements. "We're all set for AS 516, boarding should be at about 6:00 p.m. My father insisted we fly home first class," said Forrest with a little devilish grin on his face.

Chapter 54
Lynnwood Arrest

"LADIES AND GENTLEMAN, THE Captain has signaled that it is now okay to use approved electronic devices."

Forrest had taken the window seat, and Christie settled in next to him on the aisle, while Shaun had a seat in row two right behind Forrest. Christie had secured her 40mm Glock in her carry on, and she always felt more in control when she had a aisle seat. It was Friday night, and Forrest looked forward to a couple of drinks and some quality time with Christie.

"What are you working on, Mr. Drummer?" asked Christie as she leaned over and put her hand on Forrest's arm. Forrest was thinking about last night and how she had called him after dinner for a rendezvous . They spent almost two hours together down in the Silver Cloud wine bar lounge. Forrest could not remember the last time that he had connected so well with someone. Not only did they share their favorite music, food and vacation spots, they also talked at length about their families and careers.

"I am trying to come up with the lyrics for a new song," he answered.

"What comes first?" inquired Christy, "the music or the words?"

"You have to remember, I am a drummer. I feel song writing is easier for Shaun and Leon, and also Leatha. They can play a cool melody on the guitar or with Leatha on the keyboard, and then after they get a good melody, they can try and get lyrics to fit. I try and come up with words for the first verse, and then add the music and go back and find the rest of the lyrics that I think will fit into the music." explained Forrest. Forrest continued to share his philosophy that a good band goes through four stages. "The first stage is cover or garage, that is when the band just plays or covers the music that others have written. Once we have some of our own music, we can transition to a regional band. When Purple Cinnamon has twenty songs that we have written, we have the chance to get some gigs out of our region, that is a big milestone. The fourth stage is when the band has enough revenue coming in that we can hire a road manager and have a quality booking agent."

Hal made one more effort to rattle the cage of the guy who was holding up the release of the Dupree death claim check. The three hour time difference from the west coast to the east coast meant that the jerk was probably already at home. "If I could just break one of those cases loose I would have the financial staying power to wait out the other two," he said out loud to himself. Maybe tonight he would go home, have dinner, and find some excuse to sneak away to the Lotus Girl. Looking out his office window he watched with amusement as three Issaquah Police cars drove down the entrance into the business park.

Twelve hundred miles south, the Century Station of the L.A. Sheriff's department was the staging center for the pending arrest of Paco Tinson. Orange County Detectives Bobby Morgan and Frank Urqheart had just pulled into the station with the arrest warrant in hand. Two detectives had Tinson under surveillance while the rest of the arrest team were waiting for Morgan and Urqheart. Morgan and Urqheart entered the Century Station in Lynwood and were quickly escorted to the conference room. It was agreed that they and one detective from homicide and two uniformed L.A. deputies would meet up with the two detectives watching Tinson and make the arrest.

Morgan and Urqheart had in their possession the arrest warrant for Paco Tinson. Because they were not certain that Tinson would be at work, they wanted to get a warrant and be safe. The police can arrest someone without an arrest warrant, for several especial exceptions. One of those exceptions is when law enforcement officers observe you committing a crime. If a suspect is in their own home, the police cannot enter their home to execute an arrest, because of the king of the castle rule. The 4th amendment is very specific that a man's home is his castle, therefore police need an arrest warrant if they want to enter a suspect's home and make a arrest.

Tinson was removing some graffiti near the skateboard sculpture when Morgan and Urqheart and the three L.A. Sheriff's Deputies approached. The two uniformed deputies knew Paco because he was a Lynwood city employee, so they were able to point him out to the Orange County Detectives.

Morgan took the lead and asked Tinson if he was Paco Tinson. "Yah, and who are you?" mumbled Tinson as he realized that seven cops had surrounded him. The L.A. Sheriff's Deputy slid behind Paco with his handcuffs ready.

"I am Detective Morgan and we have an arrest warrant for your arrest for the murder of Fred Dupree." While the homicide detective hooked him up, Frank Urqheart read Tinson his Miranda rights.

When Bobby Morgan felt certain that Tinson had not left the area and that he and Frank were probably going to be able to serve the warrant, he called for a Orange County patrol car. He wanted to be able to transport Tinson to the Orange County jail in the standard Dodge Charger equipped with the suspect transport enclosure. Detective Morgan called for the unit to meet them at the skateboard park. Bobbie and Frank frisked Tinson and placed him handcuffed in the back of the Orange County Sheriff's Patrol Car. The five personnel from the L.A. Sheriff department said their goodbyes and left the Orange County team to deal with Paco.

Frank and Bobbie were following the patrol car on the 91 Freeway when they called Lt. Genito with the good news. Genito congratulated them and provided them with an up-date on the Issaquah arrest. "I just spoke to the Issaquah P.D. and they are on the way to serve their warrant on Ruhall. I will leave a message for Detective Cloud about your success; she should be in the air as we speak. See you guys when you get in, I am sure Tinson will lawyer up the minute he is booked. I will let the D.A. know that you're inbound." Vince Genito also asked when they thought they would arrive and then hung up.

"Bobbie, have you had any contact with Sergeant Simcic in the last few days?"

"No," he answered, "Simcic kind of painted himself in a corner with his insistence that the Dupree kid was the perp. I know he took a few days off, my guess is he is just embarrassed that he got this one wrong and Cloud and Anderson were right."

Hal Ruhall watched one patrol car peel off and drive to the back of his building, the other two cars seemed to pull up in front of his unit.

Chapter 55
Instincts

"CHRISTIE, LET ME BE direct, when the dust clears, and you and your partner get to close the Ruhall case, will you let me take you to dinner and stuff?"

Christie reached over and put her right hand on Forrest's thigh, "Forrest we do not need to wait tell the case closes and we can skip the dinner and just jump to the stuff, if you know what I mean?" She then moved her right hand up under his chin and brought his head forward until their lips met in a very serious kiss.

Hal Ruhall had always been a big believer in the power of instincts and felt that most people ignored one of their most powerful attributes. His fast and successful rise in the life insurance business was due in part to his uncanny ability to trust his instincts. When he was building his first agency, he used his judgment and instincts to hire successful life insurance agents. His four year retention of new agents was double the industry average.

When he was promoted to a Regional Vice President, he used this skill, and his instincts, to weed out his weak General Agents and replace them with a more productive team. These skills propelled Hal to the senior home office positions.

This Friday afternoon, he watched as four of Issaquah's finest headed to the entrance of his suite. Hal was no fool. He knew that the delay of the death claim checks were unusual. He did not need his survival instincts to tell him that his big gamble had failed. The great Harold Ruhall had made a high risk roll of the dice and he now knew he had lost. Hal had always called his administrative assistant Mrs. Coke. Today would be no exception, "Mrs. Coke, it appears we have guests, please tell them to come in, I am expecting them."

Detective Moran had the warrant so he was the first to enter Hal's office. He had expected a regular size executive office, but was surprised at the size and opulence of the suite. Wall after wall were covered in a life time of business achievements. Moran allowed his eyes to scan a wall with a minimum off twenty pictures of Ruhall with national celebrities, including pictures of Ruhall with Bush 41, Clinton, and Ford. What Moran did not see was Harold Ruhall reach under his desk for his briefcase.

"Mr. Ruhall, we have a warrant for your arrest, would you please…"

Inside an office, even a small handgun can create an enormous noise. A 45 Caliber Colt revolver, even when placed in one's mouth, can be, and was, deafening. The limited edition Leroy Neiman that was behind Hal's desk was now covered in blood, bone fragments, and brain matter.

Chapter 56
First Degree Murder

"Why wouldn't we push ahead for the death penalty?" questioned Senior Assistant District Attorney Marc Innis. The Assistant DA was at the Saturday morning meeting, along with Detectives Anderson and Cloud, Lt Genito and Sergeant Simcic. The Assistant Sheriff was also in the conference room.

"Look," interrupted Christie, "we have him pretty solid on the Dupree, but Flaggs and Thigpin are circumstantial as of now. My question is, would we cave in on the special circumstances and settle for just first degree with life, if he confessed to all four murders?"

There are over seven hundred inmates in California awaiting their death sentence. The charge of first-degree murder can be enhanced to life with no possibility of parole or a death sentence. The enhancements are the results of allegations of special circumstances. There are a dozen or more circumstances that can result in a penalty of life without parole or death, such as multiple murders or a contract killing.

During the conference Sergeant Simcic continued to be withdrawn and almost detached.

Lt. Genito reminded everyone that Issaquah could only keep the cap on Ruhall's suicide through today. "Today, Tinson does not know that his father is dead, but his attorney will find out and tell him in the next twenty-four hours." Genito also mentioned that Tinson called his lawyer last night. "The guys name is Lincun Marshall, a partner in a medium small firm in LA. called Coopers, Marshall and Pierce. Marc, have you heard of Marshall?" inquired Lt. Genito.

"Vince, I know of the firm, mostly criminal defense, but I do not know Lincun Marshall." responded the S.A.D.A.

"Christie, you and Marc get started this morning on Tinson. Maybe we will get a break from Bobbie and Frank, they are going through Tinson's apartment and Issaquah is working on Ruhall's stuff in his office and home."

The interrogation room was empty when the deputies brought Paco Tinson over from his cell. Christie and Marc waited a few minutes and then entered the room. Paco was seated at the table. "Mr. Tinson, we have met before, but again I am Detective Cloud and this is Senior Assistant District Attorney Marc Innis." Christie continued, "I understand that you have called your attorney, and that yesterday you were read your Miranda rights, is that correct?"

"Yes, and I want my attorney present before I talk to you guys."

"Mr. Tinson, we understand that Mr. Marshall will be here in about a hour, so we will not ask you any questions until he is present, but Mr. Innis would like to provide you some information so you can have a better conversation with your lawyer," said Christie.

"Mr. Tinson, Monday morning we will have your arraignment, at that court appearance I will formally charge you with first degree murder with special circumstances. Later I will make a decision whether to ask for the death penalty or life in prison without eligibility of parole. What I want you to discuss with your lawyer is the intelligence of confessing to your four murders in lieu of death row," explained the representative from the Orange County District Attorney's Office.

"Christie, I am going to run over to the office for a while, and call the District Attorney—he wanted an update. See you in a hour."

"Sandy, I am coming over. Marc and I have about forty-five minutes before Tinson's lawyer arrives. Try and get update from Bobbie and Frank," Christie said on her cell phone as she left the interrogation area of the county jail.

Chapter 57
Ruhall's Office

SANDY HAD BEEN IN contact with Detective Moran who had been working most of the night and morning at Ruhall's office. The medical examiner had removed Ruhall's body and the detective had been going through his computer and file cabinet. Sandy placed another call in anticipation of Christie's need for more evidence. "We are just getting started with his computers and papers, but here are some updates. We have four emails from his home computer, three of them used the name Paco, and referred to a package that had been sent. The fourth email just said 'Paco, call me from dump phone, Dad.' We found a recent report from a consultant that said that Ruhall's clients were going to live too long and that his company was going to run out of money unless some policies paid off. We also found some bank statements that show three large cash withdrawals in the amounts of $20,000, $40,000 and $50,000. Sandy, these withdrawals are all in the last three weeks. Give us the rest of the weekend and I am sure we will find some more good stuff."

A few minutes later, Christie entered the homicide unit and joined Sandy at her workstation. "Let's call Bobbie and see what they have," said Christie as she called detective Morgan.

"Christie, remember Tinson said he was playing poker with four of his friends the night of the Flagg murders. Three of those guys are in the system and we show the same tattoo on two and Tinson has the same Tat. A little art work and the letters F-T-C. We can't find it in the gang database and our gang guys do not think it is a Lynwood gang. We are going to locate one of the guys in a few minutes. Also we found absolutely nothing in Tinson's apartment, with the exception of three new disposables, bought at a local Rite-Aid."

Disposable cell phones could be purchased at most Wal-Marts and retail drug stores. They cost between ten and one hundred dollars depending on how many minutes of time you wanted. One did not even need a credit card, since you could purchase a dump phone with cash.

"Bobbie, if you get anything with your meeting with Tinson's gangbanger friend, let me know ultra fast. Thanks, and you and Frank are doing great."

"Christie, I think Tinson had a low profile gang. I don't know what F.T.C. means, but there is a connection," explained Sandy.

"Hi guys, good job in Seattle, too bad that Issaquah could not have stopped Ruhall from eating his gun," said Serheant Mike Simcic as he approached both Christie and Sandy.

"Hi Sarge," replied Christie.

"Look, I remember this Paco Tinson kid from my days in Stanton," added Simcic. "I remember he is a pathological liar. Do not believe a thing he says. I think he might be nuts," added the Sergeant. Sergeant Simcic then turned and walked out the door of homicide.

"Christie, what the hell was that about, it's Saturday, and we have not seen him in days?"

"He was at the morning meeting, but he never said a word," replied Christie. She then said, "I am going to get some coffee and carbs, the DA and I could be in for a long afternoon once Tinson's legal arrives."

"If we get anything good from Bobbie or Issaquah, I will call," yelled Sandy as Christie headed to the coffee machine.

Chapter 58
Fuck The Cops

"BOBBIE, I THINK I remember this Jose Banter." said Frank Urqheart as they drove to the last known address of Paco Tinson's poker alibi. "When I was working for the L.A. Transit Authority, just before their police department was turned over to the Sheriff's department, I remember busting him for dealing on the downtown buses. His father was a banger, and was popped in a drive by about five years ago. He was not a bad kid, just a gang wannabe," explained Frank.

"Jose Banter, Sheriff's department, open up," spoke Frank. Surprisingly the door opened and Detective Urqheart recognized a much older Jose Banter. "Jose, it's been, several years, this is my partner detective Morgan, can we talk?"

"Guys, I clean now, what's up?"

"Jose, either invite us in, or step outside, but we need to ask you a couple of questions. We can't leave until we talk," continued Frank.

"There is a table out back, the front yard is too public." replied Jose.

The back yard was small, but well maintained. The three sat down at an outdoor table, the kind of wood table you would find at a pizza place. "Jose, your buddy, Paco Tinson has fucked up badly and I am afraid he is trying to take you down also." explained Frank, "We got

Paco in lock-up for first degree murder, and it looks like he is trying to drag you and the F.T.C. guys in on the party."

"Murder, bullshit—we used to sell some pills, but that's it."

"Jose, here is the deal. We tracked Tinson by his cell phone, we know he was in Laguna Woods, yet he says he was playing poker with you. We know he left the poker party and drove to Laguna Woods. Jose, I wanted a chance to keep you off the accessory to murder list."

"Officer, this is bullshit, I am trying to go straight. I don't want any problems."

"Jose, you already have a problem, Paco pulled you into his problem, we can't un-ring that bell. Let us help you," added Frank.

"Guys, my mom and I just found out that my sister Aleta, she is 16, has leukemia. When I heard the news, I promised my mom that I would stay clean, and be here to help my sister."

"Jose, how long has it been since your father was killed, five years right? If you want to help your sister, then you need to let us help you," added Frank. "Did Paco leave the poker party and drive to Orange County?" followed up Frank. Bobbie felt that the kid was going to break, he seemed like he was ready to cave.

"If I turn on Paco, I will be dead in a week, how does that help my sister?" said Jose as he stood up from the table and threw his hands in the air in exacerbation.

"Paco has turned on you, if you don't help us you will get a minimum of five, maybe fifteen," explained Frank. "We don't want you killed, we will figure out how to keep you behind the scenes.

"Yes, Paco left the poker game and was gone for over four hours."

Bobbie and Frank spent another five or ten minutes talking to Jose before they got up from the wood table and started to leave the back yard.

"Jose, just one more thing. Confidentially - what does F. T. C. stand for?" asked Bobbie just before he opened the side yard gate.

"Confidentially – F. T. C. stands for fuck the cops!" answered Jose as he walked to his back door.

Chapter 59
Lincun Marshall

LINCUN DID NOT MIND spending his Saturday in a police station interrogation room; he thought of it as his union dues. Why have negative thoughts about something that came with the territory? He remembered the story he heard about the Ob/Gyn doctor who was talking to his psychiatrist. The doctor said he loved working with the mother in her final trimester; he loved his Ob/Gyn job. He loved helping the mother relax before her delivery; the doctor told his shrink that he had the best job in the world. And when he had a Caesarean delivery, that was the best - again he told his psychiatrist that he loved his work, but there was one thing he did not like. What is that asked his psychiatrist? The doctor said did not like babies.

Lincun Marshall loved criminal defense, and he did not mind all the hours spent in city and county jails talking to many really bad people. He had graduated from college with a Political Science Degree from U.C.L.A. and then he was accepted in Loyola Law School. He received his J.D. when he was twenty-five and the following year he passed the California Bar. Lincun Marshall's first stop, which lasted eight years, was to be one of a thousand Deputy District Attorneys with the Los Angeles District Attorney's Office. When you include the three hundred investigators and eight hundred support personnel, you have the nation's largest local prosecutorial agency with a total staffing over two thousand two hundred.

His first move to the private sector was with a large Southern California criminal defense firm. Two years later, Lincun was courted by a small upscale legal boutique called Coopers and Pierce. In just two and a half years, gross revenues had doubled and the firm's name was changed to Coopers, Marshall and Pierce.

"Paco why did you call my firm and why did you ask for me?" Paco shifted in his chair while his involuntary tic again caused his chin to jerk toward his right shoulder, Mr. Marshall, I read where you were able to get an acquittal for a member of The County Bad Kids on a multiple murder charge."

"Yes, that was our firm. Mr. Tinson, Monday you are going to be charged with first-degree murder, either at that arraignment or later the D.A. will add special circumstances. The D.A. may press for a death penalty. You have a big hole to dig out of. If anyone can help you it is my firm. We are good, but we have our rules. If you do not agree with our rules, I will walk and you will not be billed for this visit. Paco do you want to hear the rules?" asked lawyer Marshall as he leaned toward Paco and looked him straight in the eyes.

Paco answered, "Yes sir!"

"Rule one, you will not talk to the press, media, D.A.'s office including investigators, fellow prisoners and any law enforcement people, without our firm present. Rule two, we are the best, but expensive. My billing rate is $425 and our legal assistants bill out at 125 per hour. If you retain our firm, we require a twenty thousand dollar non-refundable retainer by Tuesday of next week. Rule three, no drugs while we represent you, we need you mentally sharp at all times." Mr. Marshall leaned back and waited for Paco's response. "Sir, I agree to your rules, what is next?"

Detective Cloud and Senior Assistant D.A. Innis walked into the small interrogation room and took the last two chairs. "Do we have an approximate time for Monday's arraignment?" Marshall asked the S.A.D.A.

"We are shooting for 9:30 a.m." Marc Innis then spent some time explaining to the defense attorney that the County felt that they had plenty of facts to make a case for special circumstances.

"Can we start at the beginning, why was my client arrested?"

Christie walked Lincun Marshall through the basics of the case, she did not want to show all their cards, but she wanted to give enough information so as to head off a motion for dismissal on Monday. She provided Marshall with the name of the companies that had purchased the three policies. Christie told Lincun Marshall the fact that all three of the murder victims had sold their policies to the Ruhall Settlement Group. The four emails from Ruhall to Paco, and Paco's fingerprint found at the scene of Fred Dupree. "We will be more specific when the charges are filled Monday, but suffice it to say, we will present a case of contract murder against Mr. Tinson." Christie then asked Marc Innis if he wanted to add anything.

"Counsel, as a courtesy, I want you to know, that Monday I will ask the judge that Mr. Tinson be held without bond. Also let me be direct, Monday, we will file charges that include the murders of Fred Dupree, Harvey Flagg, Victoria Flagg and Steven Thigpin. This will easily fit special circumstances and the death penalty. If Mr. Tinson pleads guilty to all four murders before next Friday, we will take the death penalty off the table and settle for life without eligibility of parole." explained the prosecutor.

"Thank you both, I would now like a few minutes with my client, and I will then see you both Monday morning." said Lincun Marshall as he stood up and shook the hands of Christie and Marc.

After the prosecutor and detective had left the room, Lincun sat back down and asked Paco one question.

"Paco, who is Harold Ruhall and the Ruhall Settlement Group?"

Chapter 60
Brother in-law Glen

ROUND TABLE PIZZA HAD just delivered a King Arthur Supreme and a dozen chicken wings to Forrest. He promised himself, that he was going to stay home and catch up on some needed sleep. While opening a bottle of red wine, Forrest allowed his mind to review all that happened Friday. When their flight landed, Christie was notified of the suicide of Hal Ruhall. On the ride from Orange County Airport Christie explained that Ruhall's death would mean a change as to how Tinson would be interrogated. She explained to Forrest and Shaun that her original plan was for the D.A. office to offer Tinson a reduced charge if he would flip on Ruhall.

When a prosecutor has co-defendants that are both charged, it is sometimes possible to get one co-defendant to agree to a lesser charge in exchange for that defendant's testimony against his co-defendant.

Forrest was so wound up last night that sleep was impossible. He had spent several hours telling Leatha and then Leon about all the action in Seattle. After a couple of hours of staring at the celling, he got back up and tried to work on the band's new song. With a glass of wine and two pieces of pizza under his belt he decided to call Christie and find out if she was able to meet with Tinson.

"Forrest, I think our prosecutor is going to have his hands full with Tinson's lawyer." said Christie. "His name is Lincun Marshall, god knows how Paco found this guy. He is first class." added Christie.

"What makes you think he is that good?" responded Forrest.

"First he pulled off a miracle last year, he was able to get an acquittal for a real bad gang leader. He is different, so many of these criminal defense attorneys are over aggressive and very flamboyant. They like to enter the interrogation room and go super alpha dog - lots of threats and the waving of the arms." Forrest, this guy shows up Saturday, white shirt, mono-color tie and very good looking."

"Now I am jealous and we have not had an official date yet," interrupted Forrest.

"Relax, that is how I describe a guy who comes across as very businesslike. I call this type a duck." Christie continued. "He is calm and quiet above the water, but what you can't see is under the water, like a duck his feet are going a million miles a hour. This guy is going to be a tough adversary."

"If you need a break tomorrow, Purple Cinnamon is going to have a practice at one in the afternoon, we will go for about two hours and then I am going to barbecue some steaks."

"Sounds cool, I will try and get through this big pile of paperwork tonight and in the morning. The good news is that so much of the forms and reports are online so I can work from home and don't need to go to the office. I will know by eleven and will give you a call."

Forrest and Christie spent another half hour or so talking about the many things that they had in common. It was clear that there was some good chemistry going on between them.

It had only been twenty-four hours since the Chief of Police had called her cell. Maureen did not have any idea how Chief Scioscia had got her number. He was very sensitive and tried to be very delicate when he told her that her husband had taken his own life. Maureen went through a dozen emotions. First she was in denial, then she had a wave of anger at her husband. After the reality of the situation set in, she felt a lot of sadness for her former husband. Thirty years of success in the business world, and it ended in suicide. After she hung up from the Issaquah Police Chief, she turned to her sister Monica, and said, "Sis, am I broke? What is going to happen? I have no idea how leveraged we are."

"Glen and I will help you get all this sorted out." Monica answered. "Maureen, Glen is going to take a couple of weeks of vacation and jump in and help you with Hal's business situation and is also available to help you with your current financial situation," her sister Monica volunteered. This was a relief for Maureen. Her sister Monica and her husband Glen were well off financially and she had absolute trust in her sister and brother-in-law. Glen was a C.P.A. and had done his share of forensic accounting. If anyone could unravel her money situation, Glen could.

"Monica, I just had a funny thought. If it turns out that I am broke, I wonder if I could get a job at The Lotus Girl?"

Chapter 61
Sweet Child O' Mine

LEATHA ARRIVED EARLY AND her husband Mitch was with her. This was unusual because Sunday was a day that most realtors put on their open houses. Forrest helped Mitch carry the Roland 700NX keyboard up to the music room. Earlier in the day, Christie had called and said she would come by about two p.m. Forrest had made a Costco run and had picked up eight ribeyes. Considering the distraction during the last couple of weeks, it was a good practice for the Purple Cinnamon band.

"The Wednesday after next, I have scheduled some time at the Fullerton recording studio." Forrest told the band. "We are hoping to lay down a master recording of our new song 'Control What You Can Control.' Please keep that afternoon clear." Purple Cinnamon spent the last twenty minutes of the practice working on Leatha's list of songs that that still needed perfection.

Leatha had wanted the band to add Guns N' Roses' 'Sweet Child O' Mine' for many months. The song was part of G.N.R.'s Appetite for Destruction album and song lore said that Axl Rose wrote the song in five minutes after he heard Slash goofing around with a riff and liked the flow. Leatha became addicted to the song after she heard Sheryl Crow's cover in 1999.

Shaun starts out in D-flat at the start of his guitar solo and changes to the key of E-flat minor.

Leatha does her best Sheryl Crow imitation as she sings,

> "Oh oh oh
>
> Sweet Child o' mine
>
> Oh oh oh oh
>
> Sweet love of mine"

Forrest had watched Steven Adler on the drums play the song over and over. This drum fill by Adler was a rock classic along with Slash and the famous guitar riff.

Forrest starts out on beat one, with the hi-hat and also the bass, and then the snare and crash at the end of the beat, and back to the hi-hat for the start of beat two.

"Guys, it is Leatha's call, but I think we are ready to move 'Sweet Child O' Mine' from almost ready to ready." explained Forrest. "Let's have a barbecue."

Before Christie left to drive home, she cornered Leon and told him, so everyone could hear, that Carol was sad that he did not join Forrest and Shaun on the last Seattle trip. "Let's drink to Gigi," proclaimed Leon.

After Christie headed home, Leatha and her husband received a call on a counter offer on one of their listings. "We need to swing by the office and respond to this offer," said Leatha as she gave everyone a goodbye hug.

Leon and Shaun stuck around while Forrest brought them up to speed on the next legal steps on the Ruhall case. "Leon, you should have seen Christie at the Starbucks meeting with Ruhall's wife. It was the turning point, and the emails that the Issaquah cops got from his computer were the smoking gun with respect to Paco Tinson. Christie, promised to call me after the arraignment tomorrow morning." explained Forrest.

Forrest then kicked around a couple of ideas with Leon and Shaun about what to do with his father's house, car and belongings. About an hour later everyone went home and Forrest did the last part of the cleanup.

Paco Tinson finished his sixth jail meal. The last time he was arrested was two years ago, a misdemeanor for possession with intent to distribute. That case was dismissed for lack of evidence. He had his doubts that his godfather could make this problem go away. It was about six years ago when he was approached. "Paco, do you know what a godfather is?" he was asked, "A godfather is a secret weapon on the inside, kind of a get out of jail free card." That was six years ago, and he had used his get out of jail free card only once, two years ago. Like magic, the evidence on his possession charge got lost.

Chapter 62
Arraignment

MONDAY WAS ALWAYS A hectic day in the judicial system, because of the arrests on Friday and Saturday. The felony arraignment would take place in Superior court before a magistrate and was the first opportunity for the defendant to receive a formal copy of the official criminal complaint. The felony complaint would include notations of jurisdiction, the parties, the statement of facts and the cause of action. The cause of action is the specific list of each crime and a citing of the specific state law that pertains to each crime.

Paco Tinson was dressed in the jail's customary orange jump suit with the letters Central Jail on the back. He had been handcuffed and was led down to the tunnel that ran under Flower Street from the Central Jail to the Justice Center. He was held in the holding facility. At about 8:30, the deputies brought a group of eight prisoners from holding to the cage.

When the judge called Tinson's case, Marc Innis had been sitting next to Christie. He joined Paco's attorney Lincun Marshall at the front of the courtroom, and then Marshall walked over to the screen by the cage that held the prisoners who were to be arraigned. Defendant Tinson was moved up to the front of the cage and seated in a chair near the security screen. Judge Jacobsen briefly explained the process of the arraignment and said she wanted to make sure that Mr. Tinson understood his constitutional rights.

The criminal complaint, in its statement of fact, went into great detail, explaining that Harold Ruhall had contracted with his son, Paco Tinson, to murder Fred Dupree, Harvey A Flagg, and Steven L Thigpin. During the crimes, Victoria Flagg was also murdered. Harold Ruhall commissioned the murders for economic gain.

The cause of action part of the complaint was very detailed and contained twenty-seven specific crimes. In addition to the four murder charges the complaint also included torture, cruelty to an animal, breaking and entering, and providing false information to law enforcement. After the complaint had been read, Judge Jacobsen then asked defendant Tinson how he pleaded.

Defense Attorney Marshall then whispered to his client who then said, "Not guilty, your Honor."

When the judge completed the complaint portion of the hearing, she then asked the defendant if he wanted to waive his right to a speedy trial.

In California, a felony case needs to go to trial within sixty days after the defendant pleads not guilty. Lincun Marshall had explained to Tinson that his defense would be very through and his firm was not going to be ready in two months. "Your Honor, Mr. Tinson would like to waive his right to a speedy trial."

Judge Jacobsen then asked the prosecutor his position with respect to bail. "Your Honor, because of the charge of first degree murder with special circumstances, the fact that the defendant is a member of a criminal gang, the multiple murder charges, the state feels that Paco Tinson is a danger to the community and with the state considering asking for the death penalty, we feel that Mr. Tinson is a flight risk. We are asking, your Honor, that the defendant be remanded without bail." Marc Innis then stepped back and looked over at Marshall. Even Marc was impressed with the way that Marshall carried himself. His slender six foot plus frame was coffered in a dark blue custom suit, white button down shirt and a solid teal tie. The only thing that Marc did not like was Marshall's hair that was dark brown and combed straight back.

The defense attorney took a half step toward the bench. "Your Honor, with the upmost respect for Mr. Innis, we feel that a mistake has been made with respect to the character of Mr. Tinson. Mr. Tinson did have a few brushes with the law in his early years, but your Honor, Mr. Tinson's record has been spotless for half of a decade. For the last five years, Paco has been a loyal employee of the City of Lynwood. His

Mother who is in this court today is dependent on his income from the Park and Recreation Department. Considering that Mr. Tinson has been part of the Lynwood community his whole life, we feel that being released with a monitoring device would be appropriate. Judge Jacobson gave Marshall a little smile, and finally said, "Bail will be set at two million dollars."

"Mr. Marshall I understand that you have an additional matter that you would like to bring before the court."

Christie was listening to the Judge and was certain that the defense was going to ask for the customary fifteen days for the filing of defense motions. She knew that it was very rare that a motion could be researched and prepared in time to be articulated at the time of arraignment.

Lincun Marshall had not gained his reputation as a top tiered defense attorney by being anything less than bold. "Thank you, your Honor. The defense is presenting a motion to dismiss, with respect to all charges that pertain to the death of Fred Dupree. The complaint citation is very specific, in that it references evidence found at the scene of the Dupree homicide." For the next fifteen minutes, Marshall cited various cases, where latent fingerprints were declared to be inadmissible because of a broken chain of custody, or problems at the assigned crime lab. Lincun then referenced a set of recommendations and suggestions made by the standards task force of the California Association of Crime Laboratory Directors. When the Orange County Crime Lab was evaluated, the task force expressed concern with training in instrument analysis and the need for adequate training in latent print analysis and crime scene investigation. When Tinson's defense attorney was finished presenting his motion to dismiss, he then thanked the judge.

"Well Mr. Marshall, I am sure that the court has not heard the last of this issue, but the motion to dismiss is denied."

After customary court business was completed, including dates to hear other motions, Judge Jacobsen called for the next case. While sheriff deputies led Paco Tinson to the back of the courtroom cage, Marc Innis walked over to where Christie was still sitting.

The Senior Assistant District Attorney leaned over and whispered in Christie's ear. "Detective, I have not seen a motion to dismiss in a felony case, and especially a murder one case in five years. My dear, your Mr. Marshall has balls bigger than an elephant. We certainly have our hands full. Let's get out of here."

Chapter 63
Cruelty to an animal.

PACO READ AND RE-READ the formal complaint. He was more pissed at himself then he was scared. He prided himself on his discipline and check lists, so how did he drop one of those envelopes at the Dupree house? One of the first things he learned during his first arrest was that the cops will lie, but this fingerprint shit is real. He had three envelopes and he did not protect them from his fingerprints because he thought he had picked them all up. He went to all that trouble with the phony evidence and then he left a print.

Twenty seven different crimes were spelled out in his complaint. He read each cause of action one more time, and wondered how they came up with this much crap. Why can't they just say he shot four people? Breaking and entering, assault, torture, and even cruelty to an animal. The one that really bugged him was giving false information to a public safety official. He threw the papers on the floor and sat on his jail bed. He was supposed to have a meeting in a hour with his attorney, maybe he would tell him about his get out of jail free card.

Sandy was going over with Christie the information that Morgan and Urqheart had dug up in Lynwood. Getting his gang bang brother to refute Tinson's alibi was a huge break. "Sandy, the biggest problem with the Jose Banco declaration, is how do we use it, without Tinson finding out? We have no way to protect Banco." Christie explained with frustration.

Sandy replied, "It's kind of a catch 22 issue. Tinson uses his guys as a alibi and they become accessories to murder, if they come clean, as Banco has done, then the gang will retaliate."

"I have an idea," said Christie. "Maybe Morgan and Urqheart could have a come to Jesus meeting with the three other gang brothers. If he can convince the core part of F.T.C. to not take a fall for Tinson, then Jose Banco might not be a target.

"Look at this, Tinson is going to meet with his attorney tomorrow and then Marshall wants a meeting between Tinson, himself, the D.A.'s office and me."

"Christie, you think Tinson heard about his dad, and wants to negotiate to avoid the needle?" asked Sandy.

"Maybe he wants a conjugal visit with you, Sandy. Let's get out of here and go get a drink," Christie volunteered.

Chapter 64
Get Out of Jail Free Card

"Your mother brought the retainer to our office this morning," Lincun informed inmate Tinson. The two were seated in the attorney interview room at Orange County's Mens Central Jail. Attorney-Client confidentiality is always a concern when a lawyer meets with his client. This particular room appeared to be well insulated and Lincun was certain that his discussion with his client would be private. A review of the charging complaint took up about a half hour of their meeting. It was after this discussion that Paco told his attorney a story that had the criminal defense attorney riveted to his chair.

"Mr. Marshall, it was six, maybe six and a half years ago that I was first approached. We had just split a big shipment of ecstasy from Belgium, into small quantities, so that none of us would be carrying more than one hundred tablets at a time. When I left this pizza place on Beach Blvd, Geno's Pizza I think, this cop comes up to me in plain clothes." continued Paco. "To make a long story short, he tells me he has had me under surveillance for a month and thinks it is time I get a godfather."

"He says that if I give him a cut of my X business, he will keep me off the legal radar." Mr. Marshall, I have been paying this guy monthly for over six years. Most of the time, I give him gold coins, I figure I have paid him close to a hundred ounces of gold. One time I got caught with some pills and was charged with possession with intent to distribute.

229

He got his hands on the evidence and my case was dismissed." Paco continued telling Lincun his relationship with this cop.

Christie had an early lunch and headed over to Central Jail to meet up with prosecutor Innis.

"Needless to say, Marshall's motion to dismiss was the talk of the D.A.'s office this morning. The best guess is that he had that motion on the shelf, and he just brushed it off and used it on us. The research was spot on, as were his case citations," explained Innis.

As Christie and Marc signed in for their meeting with Tinson, Lincun Marshall was returning from the restroom. Christie was looking for any kind of flaw in Marshall's attire, when he gave them each a warm greeting. "Would you like to get started, Mr. Innis?" Marshall said, with the charm of a seasoned politician.

Christie was the first to begin the conference. "Mr. Tinson, let me explain why we feel that our offer is worthy of strong consideration. When the jury comes in with a guilty verdict with special circumstances, you will be transferred to San Quentin and placed on death row. As you know there is currently a moratorium on California executions, and about seven hundred prisoners are cooling their heels on death row. Death row, some say is worse then death. If you will change your plea, Mr. Innis will change his penalty request to life in prison without eligibility of parole. That means you will spend your time in prison in general population.

Marc added to Christie's proposal, by sharing that they felt their case was getting stronger each day. He explained the progress in Issaquah, tracking Ruhall's payments to Paco. When he told Tinson that members of the F.T.C.s were cooperating and his alibi was gone, there was a noticeable change in the defendant's demeanor.

"Detective Cloud and Mr. Innis, we thank you for your willingness to be flexible. Something has come up that I feel will put this case in a new perspective. Mr. Tinson will you share the story you shared with me? And do not use the name or the department at this time." said Mr. Marshall.

During the next half hour Marc Innis listened intently as Christie took copious notes. Paco went into the utmost detail of his involvement with his godfather during the last six years. He even told the prosecutor and detective were he would buy the gold coins and how he would pass them to the cop. Sometimes, he explained, he would get certified gold coins that had been graded by a grading service.

Coin collectors and coin shops will send coins to independent companies that specialize in grading coins. After the coin is graded it is then encapsulated in a tamper proof container and assigned its own special certified number.

"Mr. Innis, Paco is willing to sign a declaration of fact, including the name and department of the public safety official, in exchange for a plea of guilty to second degree murder."

Christie felt that she had been given some hallucinogenic drug; her brain was numb. The representative from the D.A.s office could feel his heart beating in his chest. Marc was not sure if he was supposed to be pissed, angry or what. Finally he had gathered his thoughts.

"Mr. Marshall, I must say that the last twenty-four hours has been interesting, I would recommend that you give Detective Cloud and I, an hour or two to consider your proposal. Maybe we better make it two hours - will that work for your schedule?"

It was agreed that Mr. Marshall, Christie and Marc would meet at three thirty at the D.A.s office. Paco Tinson would be return to his cell. Paco hoped he had not missed an Orange County Jail lunch.

Chapter 65
Internal Affairs

THE PROFESSIONAL STANDARDS DIVISION of the Orange County Sheriff's Department has a staff of about fifty. The section that deals with internal complaints about employees and deputies was routinely called Internal Affairs. After leaving the jail, Christie headed directly for a meeting with Lt. Genito, while Marc hustled over to his office to update the District Attorney. The first thing that Vince Genito did after hearing Christie's version of their meeting was to call the Assistant Sheriff, and then he and Christie had a closed door meeting with Internal Affairs.

The meeting with I.A. was brief, and it was agreed that if Tinson was credible, the bad cop was most likely operating out of L.A. County. Genito promised to call if and when he found out the identity of the cop taking the bribes.

The D.A. gave full negotiating authority to Marc Innis, but did not think they should go to murder two unless it was a last resort.

The weather was perfect for the brief walk to 401 Civic Drive and the office building that housed the offices of the Orange County District Attorney. The D.A. of Orange County was an elected position, and considered an extremely desired office by those who throw their hat in the ring every four years. Lots of drama and speculation about who would run was already in the air, even though the next D.A. election was not till next year.

The conference room was a welcomed upgrade from the dull and cramped interview rooms at central jail. Senior Deputy District Attorney Marc Innis sat across from Lincun Marshall, with Christie Cloud and Lt. Genito sitting to Marc's right.

"Marc, I have written the name of the officer, who my client says has been accepting his bribes for more than half a decade. I have checked, and this member of the law enforcement community is still active. My client will testify that he was first solicited by this man, so it would appear that this is a case of extortion."

"Lincun, we have discussed your offer with the D.A." relied Marc. Christie was amused at how all the formality had been dropped and everyone seemed to now be on a first name basis. Innis continued, "If these acquisitions can be substantiated with solid proof, we are willing to drop special circumstances with all four murders, and we take the death penalty off the table."

The next hour flew by as the four negotiated and negotiated. Lincun was holding out for murder two, while Marc's last offer was murder one. Then a long discussion took place as it related to the impact of this information coming out in a jury trial. Lincun did not doubt that investigators would continue to build a very solid case against his client. If the D.A.s office and Internal Affairs spent enough time, they might find out the identity of Paco's godfather.

"Gentlemen and Lady, If the D.A. himself will support the plea deal, we will provide the name; the defendant will plead guilty to first degree-murder with eligibility for parole for the four murders and we want torture and animal cruelty both dropped from the complaint."

Marc was gone for less than ten minutes, before he returned with a sign off by the O.C. District Attorney.

"I am sure it goes without saying, that we would expect full support from this office at the sentencing hearing." added Lincun. "Oh yes, I think you will need this," said Lincun as he pulled a three by five card from his case file and pushed it across the conference room table to Marc Innis.

Lincun Marshall then got up and left the room.

Chapter 66
Gold Coins

SENIOR ASSISTANT D.A. INNIS held the card face down like he was in a high stakes poker game. He then looked at Lt. Genito and Christie while he slowly flipped over the card. With no visible reaction he then passed the card to Christie who turned it over so both she and Lt. Genito could both read the name. Christie felt a cold shiver pass over her shoulders and down her arms.

Sergeant Mike Simcic, Homicide, Orange County Sheriff Department was printed on the card. At the bottom of the card was the signature of Paco Tinson and todays date.

So many questions, so many answers, thought Christie. It was all starting to make sense. Christie thought about Simcic's strange insistence to pin the crime on Forrest. His downplaying of the evidence that pointed to Tinson. She wanted to call Sandy and Forrest so bad but she would have to wait.

Lt. Genito and Christie walked the short distance back to the department. Vince had called ahead and had set up a fast meeting with the top brass.

Two officers from Internal Affairs were in the executive conference room when Lt. Genito and Christie arrived. The Assistant Sheriff was also present. "I want a lid on this until we have a solid case." said the Assistant Sheriff. Internal Affairs said they would work ends, Simcic's financials and the gold coin connection. It was also agreed that the

D.A.s office needed to get a warrant to look into Simcic's banking matters.

For the next twenty-four hours, a minimum of ten people, five from I.A., the rest the D.A.s office were trying to verify Tinson's allegations.

The people from the D.A.'s office were able to hit a home run in Long Beach. They found a coin dealer who remembered Paco Tinson and came up with records of four PCGS certified gold coins that he had sold to Tinson last year. The PCGS grading company not only had their own number on each coin, but also had digital pictures of the coins.

Armed with a warrant, investigators from internal affairs paid a visit to the Wells Fargo branch were records showed that Simcic had an account. Not only did he have an unusual large balance in his accounts he also maintained a safety deposit box at the branch. If law enforcement has a warrant, most banks will be cooperative and open a safety deposit box. In this case, a locksmith had to drill out the lock, so the box could be opened.

The investigators took pictures of the box before, during drilling, and after drilling to maintain a chain of custody record for any evidence that was to be found. The final picture was of twenty-nine gold coins, including four PCSG certified coins.

Wednesday afternoon, in the homicide unit, had all the appearances of business as usual. Word had spread that Yorba Linda had accepted the proposal of the O.C. Sheriff Department and after twenty plus years; Brea P.D. would not be providing The City of Yorba Linda with a public safety contract. Christie wondered what would happen to the Brea Cops who would be laid off.

Sergeant Simcic had approached Christie and Sandy in the morning and assigned them to a homicide case that happened last night in Mission Viejo. The early report indicated a possible murder-suicide. While Christie was walking from room to room, Sandy was doing her own diagrams of the location of the bodies. Christie's cell rang while she was making observations in the kitchen. It was Innis from the D.A.s office, "We nailed Simcic; positive ID on Timson buying coins, and those same coins were found in his Wells Fargo box. The Sheriff told The D.A. that your Internal Affairs will make an arrest within the hour."

Sergeant Mike Simcic was getting all worked up as he lectured Detective Frank Urqheart about the problem of having women deputies,

"Dammit, Frank, If women can be as good at police work as men, then why are there no women in the NFL? It's because they are too emotional."

Lt. Genito interrupted Mike's tirade. "Mike come here a second," and Vince waved Sergeant Simcic out in the hall. Two deputies and Internal Affairs were waiting as Genito and Simcic walked out of the homicide unit door.

The last thing that Lt. Genito could hear as Mike Simcic was walked down the hall, was his ranting that, "Paco Tinson is a punk kid and liar and goddammit, if I had stayed in Oregon, I would have been Chief."

Epilogue

Maureen Ruhall felt a special relationship with Christie and called her every week or so. She told Christie that Chief Scioscia had been very understanding and helpful. She said that her brother in law had found several settlement companies that wanted to buy the corporation's life insurance policies that were still in force. Glen, her brother-in-law, thought that they would receive between two and a half to three million for the policies. Christie also learned that both insurance companies, the ones that insured Dupree, Flagg and Thigpin were probably not going to let Hal's companies profit from the murders and that the death benefits would instead be paid to surviving relatives.

Leon made a courtesy call to Gigi. He reported to the band that Carol Maddox was doing great now that she was back in branch banking, and if she ever had a vacation to Southern California, she was going to take Leon to a gentleman's club.

Lt. Vince Genito returned to Villa Park with his head held high. The City Council had caved in on the idea of getting their own police department. After hearing that Yorba Linda had changed their contract from Brea, to O.C Sheriff, Villa Park was back in the fold. The only problem was that their Chief was going to be promoted to Captain, and they were going to have to adjust to a new Chief of Police.

Purple Cinnamon had just been informed that "Control What You

Can Control" had the serious interest of Highjump Records. The record company also had heard Leatha's version of "Sweet Child O' Mine" and was going to fund a cover of the classic G.N.R. song. Forrest set up Purple Cinnamon as a California LLC, and had purchased another Roland keyboard so Leatha could have one at home, and there would be one at Forrest's house.

Sandy cozied up to Shaun and asked for some more wine. Both Christie and Sandy had locked their service pieces in the trunk of the ten passenger RSVP limo. Leon was on a blind date for the celebration. Leatha and Mitch Boseman were seated across from Christie and Forrest. The table for eight at the famous Napa Rose was feeling the good vibes. As far as Forrest was concerned there was not going to be a budget tonight. He chose the Grand California Hotel's Napa Rose restaurant, because his father had brought him there when he had sold Dupree Environmental Services.

Sandy, who was feeling no pain, announced that she had a toast. "Here is to Detective Cloud, who has just passed her Sergeant's exam. Salute!" Everyone yelled congratulations and fired back their drink.

Christie said she had just talked to Maureen Ruhall, and had some interesting information. "It seems that the law is that you cannot be the beneficiary of a life insurance policy if you are involved in the murder of the insured." Christie continued, "There is a good possibility that Forrest might receive the four million dollars from the policy that Mr. Dupree sold to Ruhall Settlement Group."

Forrest thought it was appropriate for him to make a few remarks. "It has been said, that with every adversity comes an equal, if not greater opportunity. Family is number one, no matter what the future holds; I will always remember how Purple Cinnamon never doubted me. Christie and Sandy; here is to the Orange County Sheriff's Department, and to the finest two detectives that have ever roamed the streets of Orange County. Salute."

Two hours later, their dinner was coming to a spectacular close. Christie raised her glass. "What was it that Fred Dupree used to say; for ten percent more you go first class!"

Forrest leaned up close to Christie and whispered in her ear. "Christie I love you." Christie replied, with a tiny tear in her eye, "Forrest, I love you too."

"One more thing detective, will you wear your gun to bed tonight?"

"Only if you take me back to Tacoma for a Frisko Freeze Double Cheese."